THE CHEF

(SURFER TOWN III)

REBECCA CASTLE

PROLOGUE

LOVE.

Sometimes we never see it even when we absolutely should.

We blind ourselves to it, to its possibilities, because we've been hurt before. Our past can warp our perceptions of love, make us close our eyes and shut our ears to even the thought, or chance, of it entering our lives.

And then sometimes we see only a small percentage of someone because of our blindness to love. Someone we once thought was an enemy may turn out to be our perfect partner in life. It's only because of our insecurities that we perceive them to be something they're not when, in fact, they might be everything our heart is looking for.

Sometimes we don't listen, or learn, from our heart and what it's trying to say to us because sometimes it's easier to create a false fantasy of someone than to expose our emotions. We prefer to make them the villain in our story, rather than see them as the hero we need. It's easier to hide than to love.

But sometimes you do find that person. Sometimes you do listen to your heart.

Sometimes you do see love.
And that's when it's true love.
And you should never let it go.

1

BAY

"Okay, girl. You've got this," I sternly say to my reflection in the car rearview mirror.

Nope. Not working.

I want to laugh. At myself. At my stupid attempt at being so serious and so sure of myself as I gawk in the mirror.

Because, in actual fact, I very much know that I *don't* have this.

Not at all.

I'm a joke.

I take in a deep breath and stare down at myself in the tiny mirror. My green eyes stare back at me under my brown fringe. My pale skin practically shines in the harsh Australian sunlight, and not in a good way.

Yeah, I really don't have this.

"Right, you can do this, Bay. Calm and confident, remember?" I squeak at my reflection.

Ha, I don't remember.

I take a moment to shake out the negative thoughts in my head. Then I take the keys out of the ignition and lean back in the driver's seat of my second – *most probably sixth* – hand car. I avoid my reflection and peer out the car's dirty windows at the main street of town, my focus falling on the bank opposite the parking lot.

The bank. Where I'm heading.

Here we go.

I take in another deep breath.

"You've got this," I whisper to myself, my quivering voice betraying my high levels of insecurity. "In twenty minutes' time, you'll be walking out of that bank with money in your pocket and one step closer to fulfilling your dreams."

Oh, I wish.

Okay, it's time to go in. Now or never. Suck it up, girl.

Enough sitting around in my car pretending to be an 80s self-help guru. After my little performance here in my vehicle, I think we can safely rub that off the list of potential career paths for me.

Right, stop overthinking and stop procrastinating, Bay.

Time to go in.

Might as well face the music.

I lean over to the side passenger seat and pick up the pile of papers. I skittishly thumb through the financial records, making sure everything's there and in order. This morning I had to make a last-minute quick - and extremely panicked - trip to the town's library in order to print the papers all off in time for this appointment. My brother doesn't even have a printer at his house, so it was a *very* hysterical morning trying to get everything together for this moment.

Okay, everything's here.

Good.

With another sharp inhale of air, I apprehensively open the car door and step into the hot Australian summer, locking the car behind me. I nervously cross the parking lot towards the bank, taking a quick look around the main street of town. New Water's a small place, and I've only been here for a few weeks, but even so, I've come to practically memorize all the winding streets and roads of the town. There's not much else to do here except drive around and surf, especially when you're unemployed like me.

Well, hopefully, I won't be unemployed any longer after today. Not after this appointment.

I am petrified.

I hope this goes well.

I cross the street and towards the main entrance of the bank.

As I approach the front door, leaning out to reach the handle to swing it open, someone suddenly steps in front of me, blocking me. Their hand shoots out and grabs the door handle just before I even get the chance to do so. I'm shocked by the rapid movement.

That's so rude.

I glance up to see who it is that's so abruptly cut in front of me in such a boorish and impolite way.

A man.

A guy no older than me. Twenty-seven or so. He's tall, over six feet at least, with short black hair that's wavy in that kind of classic Superman way. You know, the famous curl that falls down his forehead, the cute way he has it in the films? This guy has that. Come to think of it, his body is *also* like Superman's. Very much so. He is broad-shouldered and very muscular, just like he's straight out of a comic book. Judging by his body, he clearly spends more time in the gym than working on his manners.

A handsome man.

A handsome man who's just pushed in front of me.

"Woah." It's all I can manage to blurt out before the man quickly turns his head towards me, his brown eyes shooting sharp daggers in my direction.

He's acting as if I'm the one who's done something wrong, as if I'm the one to be so impolite.

You're the uncivil one here, mate. You've cut in front of me.

And then, as quickly as he appears, he's gone. Inside the building.

Straight into the bank without even an apology or explanation for his behavior.

"Somebody's in a rush," I murmur under my breath as I watch him scurry ahead of me.

He doesn't even hold the door open for me. It slams back with a fast swing. I have to fumble around with my documents to make sure I have a hand to stop it before the door hits me in the face.

I've not even made it into the bank, not even made it to my appointment, and I've already made a clumsy fool out of myself. Typical me.

Typical Bay Dover.

It's literally one of the most important days – *meetings* - of my life and I'm stumbling around with a bunch of papers outside the door like an awkward baby horse taking its first steps.

All thanks to this rude Superman dude.

Henry Cavill, you are not, mate. No matter how much you look like him.

I step inside the bank, trying to look as professional as ever even after nearly running headfirst into the door. I check my hair, making sure it's all still tied back in the ponytail and there are no loose strands ready to embarrass me, and I step up to the ropes. In the line for the bank teller.

I take in a deep breath.

Calm yourself, Bay. Forget about the rude man.

But I can't forget him. He's standing right in front of me in the line. All I see is his back.

The banker at the counter finishes with the person they're dealing with and calls Superman over. I take a step forward as he moves ahead. I'm next after rude boy.

If I were anywhere else, I definitely would say something to him. Make a snarky comment. Unfortunately, though, I should currently be focusing on this meeting and not on rude, handsome men.

I check down at my financial documents one last time, scanning through the pages. There's not a lot there. *Ha.* I don't really have much in the way of money. Or assets. Or property. It's just me and that rusty old car sitting out there in the parking lot.

That's all I have.

I close my eyes and pray to whoever's listening up there in the sky to just grant me one wish. That's all I want. One wish. Right now.

Hopefully, I have enough for it to work today. I wish my plan works.

If this thing today doesn't work out for me, then I'll have nothing. If the bank doesn't approve my loan application, then I might as well quit everything and go live as a crazy cat lady in a log cabin in the woods.

Please let this work. Please approve me.

I hear some sort of loud commotion in front of me. I open my eyes to see Mr. Superman himself arguing with the banker at the counter. He's the commotion. His arms are waving in the air as he argues, and the banker is completely still behind the counter, calm and staring at the muscular guy, his eyes narrowing as Superman spiels out his anger.

"What do you mean?" Fake Henry Cavill says, his voice rising so that everyone in the bank can now hear him. He wants us all to be involved in this. The banker looks down at the papers in front of him and shakes his head.

"You have only the one form filled out," the banker replies.

"What do you mean, only one form? I did what you told me to do."

The banker sighs. "You need the other one we posted to you filled out as well, not just this one."

Superman crosses his arms. His biceps pop out. Yeah, the dude's *super* muscular. He'll be kind of hot in a jock kind of way if he wasn't so effing rude. "There was another form?"

"Yes, it's made very clear on the first form that you need the second."

"Don't get all snide with me now."

"I'm not, sir."

"Well, I must've left it in my car."

The banker puts down his pen like he means business. "You can't leave the queue, sir, otherwise, your place is forfeit, and you'll have to line up again."

Superman isn't listening. "Hold on one second and let me get the document from the car."

"I'll have to serve the next customer if you do leave, sir. You'll have forfeited your place in the line if you do step out."

"Forfeit?" Superman asks, incredulous. "What do you mean? Just give me one moment and I'll get the other form from the car."

"I can't do that, sir. I'll have to serve the next customer if you do leave."

Superman turns around to check who the next customer is. When he sees it's me, his face turns red. Oh, he's not happy about that. He spins back round to the banker. "Don't you dare."

What did I do to him to make him so pissed off with me?

He's the one who pushed in front of me.

"It's the rules, sir."

"I don't care. I'm in a rush. I can't wait around all day."

"I'm sorry, sir."

I have to say, I'm kinda enjoying this little spat. Seems like karma's come round to bite Mr. fake Cavill in the ass. He shouldn't have pushed in front of me at the door like he did.

This is fun.

At least this little embarrassment I'm witnessing has put off my nerves; I'm assured that at least I'm not this guy embarrassing myself in front of everyone in the bank.

Superman points at the banker. "One second, that's all I'm asking. Give me one second to grab the other form from the car."

Before the banker can even respond, Superman spins back around and rushes past me out the bank's door, glaring at me dangerously as he passes by. I avoid his stare and I shuffle the papers in my hands. I think I have the right forms.

I hope I have the right forms.

Forget about handsome rude man and just focus on what's happening right here, right now, Bay. That's what I tell myself.

The banker locks eyes with me.

"Next," he calls out.

Oh god.

That's me.

Here we go.

My turn.

Suddenly all my nerves come flooding back as I remember how important the next few minutes are going to be. This could change my life, for better or worse.

I pray this works. It better work.

2

BAY

THIS BANKER HAS my entire future in his hands. His decision, right now, will decide my fate. For better or for worse.

It's all up to him. And what he decides right now.

Oh god.

It's terrifying.

At the counter, I nervously surrender my financial documents like they're my newborn baby. My hands shake as I rifle through the pages, and the banker takes them without a word. He sits in front of me, the bank's counter between us. A gulf.

It feels like a wall.

Everything depends on this man and his decision today.

And he doesn't seem like the most *humorous* of fellows.

"And what do you intend to do?" he asks me quietly, without making eye contact. I lean forward, trying hard to calm my shaking hands and to look professional and composed.

I am anything but.

"I'm looking to get a small business loan," I reply. "Please."

I have to add something pleasant. I hope it helps, but the banker doesn't react to my *please*.

He's like a robot. Cold and calculating.

This is who decides my future?

"And what *small business* do you intend on starting with this potential loan?"

My nerves really kick in now. I know they say it feels like butterflies in your stomach. Well, right now, it's like there's a whole *greenhouse* of butterflies trying to escape my insides.

"A baking company."

My voice comes out as a teeny tiny whimper. The banker blinks, not hearing me properly. I realize how super small my voice must've come out as.

"Pardon?"

"A baking company," I repeat a little louder, stumbling over the words. The banker seems unimpressed by my application. Or confused. I don't know which. I know I'll need to explain more. "I want to start a baking company with the loan. I love baking; it's my passion. Well, food's my passion, really. Any time of food or cooking I just love. I really think I can make a good go out of this. I've had a life-time of rocky starts and even rockier employments in so many places, so I thought *why not*, you know? Why not become a baker? It's what I'm good at. You can see I've got everything in there in those papers. A whole plan. Every-thing. I've done a step-by-step plan to make a successful business, just you look. I think I can make a really good go."

Well, that all came out in one hurried one-breath sentence.

Stop blathering on, you idiot. It isn't going to help.

For precise, concise, and to-the-point pitch speeches, I think that was the worst one in the history of pitches.

But I hope it does the trick.

Hope.

Every word I said was true, though. I love cooking and baking, and I really do think I can make a successful go out of it. Sure, I've never opened or run a business ever in my life, but this is something I'm super passionate about. Something I really believe will succeed. I've got the drive, and the energy, and the passion.

I just need the money.

I need this loan.

Please give me this loan, Mr. Banker.

Without a single word of reply to my verbal diarrhea of a pitch, the banker begins speed-reading through my documents page-by-page, flicking through each one so quickly it sets off those stomach butterflies again. I try to discern his expression, but the man is unreadable. It's a pretty good skill to have as the person who decides people's entire futures on a whim. What will he do about mine?

The banker lifts up the full glass of water that's been sitting on the counter to his lips and takes a sip as he continues reading.

This is unbearable. I can't take this suspense.

I bite my lip.

And then the bank's door slams shut behind me with a bang. I turn and look.

It's Superman.

He's back.

And, judging from the heavy frown on his face, he doesn't look happy. Not happy at all that I've taken his place. Not happy that he has to now wait for me to finish.

Well, tough. Karma's a bitch.

I watch him as he steps to the ropes that separate me -

and the banker - from the line. Superman taps his foot impatiently.

I quickly turn back to the banker. He doesn't notice Henry Cavill's return, or he doesn't care. He's too busy thumbing through my documents to worry about customers.

I hope the quick speed with which he's rummaging through my papers means something good. It's either that or something incredibly bad.

He finishes, dropping the papers on the counter, and looks down at me.

Oh.

Yep, it's incredibly bad.

I can tell.

"What is it?" I ask, my voice trembling.

But I know the answer already.

Of course, I do.

"Unfortunately, it's going to be a no from us, I'm afraid, miss – ah..."

"Dover. Bay Dover."

"Yes, like I was saying, it's going to be a *no* today."

I'm not backing down that easily.

"How can that be, though?" I ask, pointing at the documents. "Did you read everything? Did you see my step-by-step plan? I have it all there."

"I did read your plan."

"And?"

"It's not good enough, unfortunately. A plan typed up on one page isn't exactly the kind of in-depth business proposal we're looking for."

"What do you need, then?"

The banker shrugs. "More than a few pages of paychecks and a rudimentary plan, I'm afraid."

I take in a deep breath.

Think, Bay. Think clearly now. This is the most important moment of your life here.

Everything hangs on a thread, and it's slowly being cut away.

"Look, I *know* I can make this work," I say, my voice at a whisper. I don't want to cause a scene in the bank. Not like what Superman did. I need to persuade this man, not yell at him. "I have everything going for me. This is my passion. My life's work. I know I'm a good baker and a good cook."

"I'm sorry, but passion isn't a commodity we take here, Miss Dover," the banker replies, sliding my documents towards me.

I slide them back.

I really refuse to give up this easily.

"Please. I know this can work. Take a chance on me."

"It simply won't be a viable option for us, Miss Dover. You're too risky."

"Risky?"

"You have no assets, and no assets means you're too big of a risk."

"I have a car. Does that help?"

The banker sighs and narrows his eyes at me. "I doubt your car can cover even a small fraction of the costs, let alone act as a good enough asset for us to consider giving you this loan."

Well, he isn't wrong. The car isn't exactly a high-performance vehicle.

"Look, I've got no assets. I've had a tough few years. I've only just moved here to New Water as a favor to my brother. I don't have a house or a brand-spanking-new car," I say. "But I do have a heart. I do have passion. I have the determination to make this work. I know it will. Just, please, let me. A small loan, that's all I'm asking for. A few thousand dollars."

The banker tuts and shakes his head.

No.

It's like the earth below me is slowly eating away at my legs; it's like I'm sinking into the ground.

It's a no.

I see my dreams evaporating in front of my eyes.

"But..."

I begin to protest, but someone shouts behind me.

"Clearly he can't lend you the money, so how about you give up?"

It's a male's voice.

Superman's voice.

I spin around to face him.

"What?"

"He's already said the bank can't lend you the money, so go."

This bastard.

"You're incredibly rude, you know that?" I shout back, losing my composure.

This is a very important moment for me and he's ruining it.

"And you're incredibly slow," Superman responds. "I'm in a rush here, so give up and go home."

I turn back to the banker, unable to deal with that crazy man. He may look like a gorgeous prince from a fairy tale, but obviously, he is, in fact, a monster.

"Are you sure there's nothing you can do? No loan you can give me?" I ask the banker in the sweetest tone I can do. I hope I can appeal to his humanity.

Oh wait, I forgot. He's practically a robot.

He shakes his head. "Nothing I can do for you today, Miss Dover."

Footsteps approach me from behind, and before I even get the chance to turn around, Superman's voice booms next to my ear. He's stormed towards me and is now literally right over my shoulder.

"Hurry up," he says, making me jump in surprise. "I don't have all day."

He's literally right behind me. He's walked up right behind me.

Without knowing exactly what I'm doing, I spring to action. I reach for the banker's full glass of water that's sitting on the counter, grab it in one hand, spin around, and throw its liquid contents over Superman.

I don't even think, I don't even comprehend the consequences of my actions before I've chucked the entire glass over the man.

And now he is *dripping* in water.

Oh my god.

I did not intend for that to happen. It was an automatic response to him practically shouting in my ear; it was like my body was taken over by my primal instinct to defend myself.

I've just splashed water over a complete stranger.

And yet I don't feel regret.

He deserved that. One hundred percent.

Superman glares at me. He's in shock. His eyes dart from his soaking wet shirt to me, then to the empty glass of water in my hand, and then back to his shirt.

I glance back at the banker, and even he's expressing emotion on his face. The cold and calculating robot is shocked. His mouth hangs open at the sight before him.

I drop the empty glass onto the carpet, grab my documents in one go, and hastily sprint straight out of the bank before anyone, especially Superman, can react to what I've done.

I am out of there before anyone has a chance to stop me.

Holy shit.

I've just chucked water over someone. Someone who deserves it, but *still*.

In the space of a few minutes, I went from applying for a loan to pouring water over the rudest man I've ever met. A man who can crush me between his biceps if he wants.

I don't stop running until I reach my car.

3

CLIFF

"Do you need a towel or something?"

I raise my eyes from my wet shirt to the banker.

"*Very* funny," I reply, my voice bristling with anger. What a joker.

My shirt is stuck to my skin and the cold water chills my pecs. I'm freezing and the banker is just laughing at me?

Come on, man.

I'm still in shock over what has just happened. That random girl sprayed *water* over me? Like, seriously, what the fuck was that all about? She was acting like she was in some kind of film or something, snatching that glass and tipping it over my head. She even had to stand on her toes to reach my hair. That was all just super dramatic.

What a weirdo.

I turn back to the bank's door and I see no sight of her. Well, she's left in a hurry. Completely gone. And I don't blame her. If I ever get my hands on her, there'll be absolute *hell* for her to pay.

I look down at the form in my hand, the form I've just hastily collected from my car. Like my shirt, it's also wet. The edges of the paper curl up as the water soaks through. The ink's running.

The form is completely ruined. All my work filling it out literally gone down the drain.

She's done this, that pale little thing who so cheekily cut in front of me whilst I went to the car. She's got me all wet.

What a bitch.

I swivel back round to the banker. He blinks at me, also shocked by what's happened.

But not shocked enough to not utter that silly towel joke.

We stare each other down like it's a competition, and I win. He nervously looks away and I straighten up my shoulders.

Not such a joker now, hey?

"I'll be back," I growl at him before storming out of the bank. I slam the door behind me with a loud bang to emphasize how serious my threat is.

The hot Australian sun warms my wet chest as I step outside. I catch my reflection in the bank's glass windows and I can see I am clearly completely soaking wet. Dripping.

The water is also incredibly cold, and I realize the banker must've had ice in that drink.

Great.

I wipe my wet hands on my suit pants and scan around for my car. Across the street.

I head towards it, mindful of how *stupid* I must look to the other people of New Water. I've rushed out of the bank dripping with water right in the middle of the day when the main street is at its busiest. I really must look a stupid sight to everyone around me doing their shopping.

And all because of that woman.

Who is she?

She sure has a lot of balls to do what she did back in there. I'm a tall, muscular guy, but she still felt it safe enough to chuck a whole glass of water over me? In public.

And then she disappeared in a flash. *Whoosh*. She ran past me and out that bank's door like a dart.

Who is this random girl? She's spiked my curiosity.

I know a lot of people in this town, but I don't recognize her at all. I've never seen her face before around here, I'm sure of it. She's not a face I would forget lightly. Pale. Brown hair. Green eyes. A bit like that chick from *Game of Thrones*. The one with the dragons, but with her natural brown hair instead of blonde.

She's kinda pretty, in a way. She's not my usual supermodel type at all, but somehow more *real* than a lot of those shallow women I've dated.

This whole water-throwing incident? She has sass, that's for sure, and that's something that I find *very* attractive. Especially on a girl. Especially on someone who looks like they couldn't harm a fly, like her.

She still found a way to justify picking up a glass of water and throwing it over me, and that takes some balls. A pretty, sweet girl like her with that level of sass? She's an enigma.

But she's also crazy. *Super* crazy to insult me in the way she has.

Me? A Finn.

Cliff Finn.

If she actually lives here in New Water, then she should've known who I am when she saw me. She should've known I'm a Finn, and that's not something you consider lightly when you're about to throw a glass of water over a member of our family.

Yep, no one messes with a Finn, especially not in New Water.

But she did.

No, stop this.

I need to stop thinking about her. She's a nobody, even if she's got that sexy, feisty attitude and a pretty face. She's just not worth thinking about. I need to forget about what happened in that bank and just move on. There's no point in wasting my time hunting this random girl down, even if she embarrassed me in that bank, even if she is incredibly alluring.

No.

I'm not going to find her. No way am I dealing with a girl like that again, especially not after my ex.

No. I've sworn off women, especially women like this girl. Sass and all.

Screw her.

I don't want to run into her ever again, and if I did, then she'll deserve what's coming to her.

No one embarrasses me.

Especially not in New Water.

If she's spent any time here, then she'd know my reputation. She'll know not to mess with me. She'll know what I'm capable of and the power my family wields in this small town.

If we ever meet again, then she'll regret what she did there in that bank.

I flick my hands as I reach my car across the street from the bank, shaking out the built-up tension and anger from my body. She's not worth it. She's not worth my time or energy. I have far more important things to do than to think of some pretty girl and the stupid decision she made to splash water over me.

I unlock my vehicle. My car's a Lamborghini; a

powerful display of the wealth and power I have in this town.

I sit in the plush driver's seat and close my eyes, reminding myself of who I am and how I shouldn't care about some girl insulting my ego with a glass of water.

Don't worry about her. Don't even think about her anymore.

But I can't get her out of my head.

Fuck it.

I have important things to do; that'll take my mind off her.

First, I need to go home and change my shirt, and maybe even have a shower to clean off this banker's water that's currently making its way down my pants. Maybe I'll even go for a swim in the ocean. I guess that'll cleanse my mind of this girl.

Yeah, maybe I'll do that.

I open my eyes and slam my keys into the ignition.

Time to forget about that stupid girl.

4

BAY

I PARK the car outside the school gates and lean back in my seat, trying to decompress and truly comprehend what has just happened.

Holy shit.

I actually can't believe I did that. I actually *threw* water into that guy's face.

That was so unlike me.

It just happened. I had no control over my actions. My body just reacted to him coming up to me from behind like I was doing some kind of defense mechanism. Back in the bank, my hand reached for that glass on the counter instinctively and without hesitation.

I didn't *mean* for it to happen.

And that's why I ran out there and into my car.

Superman was a big guy, and I know he could've crushed me like an ant with just one of his fingers. I didn't want to face his wrath, so I bolted the heck out of there before anything could happen, before the dude could get over his initial shock.

It's okay now, Bay. You're outta there.

Yeah. I got out of that bank alive.

And now I'm at the school just in time for the end-of-day bells to ring.

I've never been that brave before.

I know throwing that water was an insane thing to do - the wrong thing to do - but, even so, sitting in my car outside the school gates, I smile to myself.

Yeah.

I was pretty badass.

It's been the one good thing to happen today. I needed it; getting rejected by the bank has completely crushed my soul, but I haven't even had time to think about that since I've nearly had a heart attack over what I did with Superman and that glass of water.

But still. I was *rejected*.

Fuck.

I get to think about it now that I'm out of danger. Now that I'm sitting alone in my car, everything comes flooding back. The banker. My documents. The way he looked at them dismissively and the way he spoke down to me as he rejected them. It was like he was rejecting me.

All my dreams went out the window. That's probably why I felt brave enough to chuck that water; I simply had nothing left in me. My dreams were shattered when that banker shook his head and told me no.

Everything I've worked for.

No loan.

No money.

How can I start a business now? I have zero money. Nada. Nothing.

I'll just have to get a job.

Well, you do have that job interview tonight.

Yeah, the job interview. That's one good thing I've got going for me now today. I did apply for a waitressing gig at some restaurant a few days ago thinking I won't even turn up to the interview because I'll be able to get the loan from the bank, but now that I don't have it, I just have to go to the interview.

Back to being a waitress once again? Here goes.

The only thing I'm good at.

RING.

I'm shaken out of my thoughts and back to the real world with the ringing of the school bells.

School day's over.

I hop out of the car and lean against its rusty frame as I take a glance into the school. The kids will be coming out in a minute. I anxiously wait to see the familiar faces of my niece and nephew come running towards the gate. The other parents wait in their cars beside me. I know a few of them, but I still feel like an outsider having only been in New Water for a few weeks.

And behind me, opposite my niece and nephew's place, is another school. Poseidon's Academy. The elite private school of the region. It's funny having two schools on the same road facing each other. The poor working-class school opposite one of the best schools in the country. One you need to re-mortgage your house to send your kid to. Poseidon's Academy has the results, though. If you want your kids to do well, then send them there.

I wish my own nephew and niece could get the chance to go there. I wish they didn't have to experience a life like mine, full of temporary waitressing jobs all over the country and crappy cars. I hope neither of them will ever get rejected for a small loan at a bank one day.

I sigh and flick my brown hair back.

Don't show them how upset you are, Bay, don't show them how your dreams were crushed today.

I've gotta stay strong for these kids, especially with what's happened to them over the last few months. It'll be unfair for them to see their aunt break down. They shouldn't see that my dreams have been utterly destroyed.

Suddenly, schoolchildren come streaming out of the school, backpacks and sports bags are everywhere. A flood of children. The air is filled with the sound of little feet running to their parents. I sit up from the car and search the crowd for my niece and nephew.

There they are.

I see Pearl's little face first. Her little pigtails dancing around as she sprints eagerly towards me, her tiny backpack flying around on her shoulders. She's so small for her age, six years old, and still a baby. She's gripping something in her hand. I see it's a piece of paper.

She looks just like her Mom.

Pearl runs right up to me, wrapping her arms around my waist in a big hug.

"Hello, Pearl," I say with a chuckle. Despite all the crap I've had to deal with today, seeing her makes my heart soar with happiness. She's so cute.

"Good afternoon, Bay," she replies in her singsong voice, an adorable little list sprinkled in.

"Hi, Bay." Davy, my nephew, suddenly appears by our side. He's older than Pearl at ten years old. He acts like her big brother as well, very protective of her.

He has to be after what they've experienced the last year.

"Hi, Davy," I reply, leaning over to rub his hair. He pokes his tongue out at me and I reply in turn. "Let's get in the car and get outta here."

I open the car door as Pearl and Davy fight to see who gets to go in the front.

"My turn!"

"No, it's my turn, Pearl."

"Let your sister sit up front," I say to my nephew, breaking up the fight before it inevitably ends in tears. Davy glares back at me with a scrunched-up face, but I nod back at him with a serious look. "You're the big brother, so that means you have to treat your sister like a princess."

He rolls his eyes, but I know he understands. He throws his bag in the back and sits in, doing up his seatbelt and then leaning forward to help Pearl with hers. He's a good boy.

"Yeah, I'm a princess," Pearl reaffirms to all of us as I turn on the car and pull it away from the curb, mindful of running over any tiny children on my way out. We reach the main road and start heading home, toward their dad's place. My brother. My new home.

"Why don't we go to the other school?" Davy asks.

"What other school? Poseidon's?"

"Yeah. They have really nice uniforms there. My best friend from primary school goes there. He says it's great and they have a really good soccer team."

Might as well be straight with him. Davy's a smart boy.

"Your dad and I just don't have the money," I reply. "It's very expensive there."

"Oh." It seems like my answer, however blunt it is, is enough for Davy. He nods and leans back into the car seat, satisfied with what I've said.

"Had a good day at school, guys?" I ask as I spin the steering wheel between my hands. The two schools disappear behind us.

"Alright," Davy grunts, reminding me how he's going to be a proper teenager in a few years with that monosyllabic response. He's definitely going to turn into a looker. I bet he's gonna break a lot of girls' hearts by the time he's in his

twenties. He's charismatic and sporty, inheriting the physi-
cality of his dad and the good looks of his mom.

Yeah, he's gonna be a real charmer.

"And you?" I ask Pearl.

"I've made a picture," she announces proudly, lifting up
the piece of paper she's been holding in her hand. I squint at
it, mindful of not taking my eyes off the road for too long.
She's applied a lot of color to her artwork and mixed a lot of
styles. Watercolor and pens and crayons. A real Picasso in
the making.

"What is it, sweetie?"

Pearl takes in a deep breath, readying herself for a little
spiel. "It's a picture of me and daddy and you and Davy."

"Aw, that's nice."

"And mommy's there too. She's in the clouds because
she is in heaven because she died."

Oh.

Hearing her say that makes my chest jump. Hearing
Pearl describe her mother's death so nonchalantly and
so *matter-of-factly* makes me want to start crying right here
and now. No child should ever have to say something like
that, especially not one as sweet, young, and innocent as
Pearl Dover.

I glimpse Davy through the rearview mirror. His face is
expressionless, but I see him gripping the car seat so tightly
that his knuckles are white. He's old enough to know. He's
old enough to understand.

Poor boy.

He won't say anything about what his little sister has
just said, but I know it affects him. Of course it would. He's
wise beyond his years; he knows the pain of losing his
mother. He's feeling it more than I am.

Pearl doesn't mean anything by it, she's just stating
facts. Her mommy did die only a few months ago from an

aggressive type of cancer. It took hold in only a matter of months. No child should see their parent fighting such a horrible thing.

The whole situation is horrible.

Every day I want to cry for them, to comfort them. The truth is that they seem to be stronger, braver, and are coping with it better than me. Better even than their dad.

That's why I'm here in New Water. Once I heard about what was happening, I packed my bags, moved out of my rented flat in the city on the other side of the country, and moved to this small town where my brother lives in order to look after my nephew and niece in their time of need. It was the very least I could do. They needed a mother, a female presence in their life, and I could provide some semblance of that.

Their dad works full time out in construction trying to put food on the table. I have to be here to make sure they get looked after while he deals with his grief and also with trying to provide. I hope I'm doing a good enough job, but I know I could never match up to their real mother. Not in a million years.

But I try my best.

"That's very nice," I say, responding to Pearl's picture. She beams at me, unaware of how much my heart is breaking for her and her older brother.

Behind us, Davy leans forward in his seat. "Do you have a boyfriend, Bay?" he asks.

"Boy, you're full of questions today, aren't you?"

Davy shrugs. "I'm just wondering. Why don't you have a boyfriend? Do you have one?"

I laugh. The question's thrown me off-guard. I did not expect to be questioned about my love life today. It's another one of the surprises of dealing with my nephew and niece. "You're too smart for your own good, you know that?"

"Answer the question."

God, he's so inquisitive and confident he should be a detective or something.

I turn my head around to look at Davy. "Where would I have the time to even have a boyfriend when I'm so used to looking after you two brats?" I reach over and tickle Pearl. She giggles as my roving fingers dance over her tummy, her pigtails dancing on her little head. She's so *goddamn* cute.

It's true though. I don't have the time to even think about a man when I'm so tied into dealing with Pearl and Davy, as well as try to set up my own baking business.

Well, that business won't even take off now, thanks to the bank.

Ugh.

I need money.

Everything hinges on this waitressing interview tonight, then. Gotta make that work. And not just for me, but for my niece and nephew and my brother. I can't stay unemployed for long.

I need a job.

5

BAY

I'M GETTING ready for the job interview when my brother comes through the front door.

And it's pure panic in the house.

I'm standing in our little kitchen, applying lipstick in the mirror, with Davy and Pearl sitting around and watching me. When we hear the familiar crunching of my brother's – their dad's – car pull up outside the house, I quickly hush them away back to their bedrooms.

"Go, guys, back to bed before he sees you."

Davy grunts and Pearl giggles as they sprint back to their rooms.

It's nearly eight and, according to their dad's instructions, they should already be tucked up in bed and definitely not playing around in the kitchen watching their aunt ready herself for an interview.

Those naughty rascals.

I do like having them around, though. They temper my bubbling pre-interview nerves with their cheeky smiles and incessant questioning over everything in the way only curious kids can. I need them to take the edge off, to calm my chattering brain as it, paranoid as it is, runs through the gauntlet of all the possible scenarios and worries about this job interview.

What if I embarrass myself?

What if I don't get it?

What if I can't find another job and therefore can't make any money?

My future seems to me like a dark abyss that I'm going to fall into, something I can't escape from.

I'm usually someone who doesn't show their emotions, who hides behind a cheerful mask, but truth be told, right now I'm scared. I'm devastated about being rejected for the bank loan, and I'm worried about what's going to happen to me, but most of all, I worry for my niece and nephew and what kind of world I'm helping to raise them into when their own aunt can't even secure a job.

So much rests on this job interview.

What a crazy day this one's turning into. I can't believe this morning I *actually* threw water over someone. It still makes me chuckle. That's one good thing to happen today, and getting rejected at the bank was the worst.

And I still have to do this job interview.

My brother, Fisher, unlocks the front door and steps inside. I stop applying makeup to glance over at him.

Those kids better be in bed now.

My brother is a tall guy. Broad and muscular. He works in construction, so he has to be. He moved to New Water nearly ten years ago with his wife, and now I live with him and the kids.

Since the passing of his wife, he's been going through a tough patch but, like me, he doesn't show it. He's a strong man having to be even stronger because of his kids. He can't show weakness around them, he can't show how shattered his world is because of what happened with their mom. He has to be brave. Strong. But inside he's hurting, I can tell. You can't hide a lot of things from your sister, especially when we're so alike. I know him too well to understand he's *really* hurting inside.

And that's why I've got to be here, to help carry his load, even though he would never admit it.

"Hi," I greet from across the room. Fisher's house is small, the only one he could afford on his meager builder's salary.

"Evening," he replies. He's still wearing his construction uniform. It's very dirty. It's been a long, hard day for him, just like many others. Fisher works overtime to make sure he can provide for his kids and for me. It's another reason why I need this job tonight. "How was the bank?"

I roll my eyes to suggest exasperation. "Terrible."

"That bad, huh?"

"Yeah."

Fisher rips off his muddy boots and squeezes past me into the kitchen, collecting a bottle of cold beer from the fridge. He gulps it down like it's the last drop of water in the Sahara. "Do you want to talk about it?" he asks.

"Not really," I reply. "I have to get to this interview soon."

"It's the evening, though. I've never heard of a job interview happening at night. You sure it's happening now?"

"Yeah, it's tonight. I double-checked the email."

"So strange. You would think now would be the busiest time for a restaurant and that they won't have time to even talk to you, let alone call you in for an interview."

I shrug. "It's the time on the email. I guess this means they're desperate for staff and that's only a good thing, right? I guess they'll definitely need me."

"Sure."

I might not seem to care as much as Fisher, but I also find it odd that the interview's happening at this time. I did do a double-take when I read their reply to my application. I did email the restaurant back, and they confirmed it was tonight.

Weird.

"At least it's an interview," I say. "We need the money."

Fisher places his beer bottle onto the kitchen counter and crosses his arms. "You know you don't need to do this."

"I do, though."

"I know you've worked so many waitressing jobs before and you didn't like a lot of them. You really don't have to do this. Look, I can work more hours at the site to get us through this."

I tilt my head at him disapprovingly. "The whole point of me being here is for you to work *less*, not more," I reply. "Fisher, you need to spend time with your kids. That's what your wife would've wanted."

Fisher bows his head, reaches for his beer, and takes another sip. "Right, as long as you're okay with working again."

"I am," I reply, smiling. My brother is a stubborn guy, but I'm more so. Ever since we were young, I was always the one to never back down. "The kids have eaten dinner and have done their homework."

"You're a star." Fisher smiles back at me.

There's movement in the doorway behind him. Pearl. She's standing in the shadows outside her room, peeking into the kitchen with her thumb in her mouth, watching her dad and me. Fisher doesn't spot her, but I glare menacingly at her. "And they should be in bed as well."

Pearl giggles at my comment aimed at her and sprints back into her bedroom.

Naughty girl, but I guess she takes after her aunt.

"What would I do without you?" Fisher asks, finishing his beer.

I give him a wink as I collect my car keys and head towards the door.

"You wouldn't be able to do anything."

"That's probably true. Have fun."

"Sure will."

Right.

The job interview.

6

BAY

THE RESTAURANT IS EMPTY.

Especially for a Friday night.

It's completely deserted.

I push through the main door and enter. Rockpool's on the main street of New Water, just down the road from the bank. I averted my eyes from that place when I drove past, not wanting to relive this morning's memories.

I'm shocked when I walk through the front door of the restaurant and look around. It is completely empty. All these tables laid out but no one sitting down. The bar is abandoned. There are no customers at all.

They must be really struggling.

Friday night and no patrons. What is going on?

I stand in the reception area and wait, but there's no host to greet me.

Should I ring a bell or something?

I am about fifteen minutes early for my interview, a

result of my energetic nerves. They control me. Maybe I'm too early, maybe this makes me seem too eager?

Calm down, Bay. Stop overthinking things.

"Hello," Someone comes sprinting down the restaurant from the kitchen in the back all the way to me standing at the front door. She's a beautiful woman with long blonde hair and a wide smile. She skips towards me, clasping her hands together when she reaches the reception.

"Hi," I reply.

"Hello," she repeats, out of breath from her quick trip from the back of the restaurant to the front. "Welcome to Rockpool. How may I help you?"

Her voice has got an accent behind it, but I can't tell from where. Maybe European?

Stay focused on what's happening right now. This interview's so important to think about what accent she has.

"My name's Bay," I say with a smile. "Bay Dover. I'm here for an interview."

The woman's eyes light up as she recognizes my name. "Ah, Bay! Lovely to meet you, I'm Dominika." She raises her hand for me to shake. "We spoke via email. Thanks for coming. You're earlier than I expected."

"Oh, is that a problem? I can wait in my car if you want."

Shit. Of course, you knew coming too early would somehow bite you on the ass, Bay.

Dominika laughs. "Of course not. Don't be silly." She waves her hand around the restaurant. "We're so quiet tonight, so how about we get started now? Come with me to the manager's office."

I follow her towards the back of the restaurant, to near the kitchens. The heat from there wafts over me and I'm reminded of all the past waitressing jobs I've had before. I'm an old hand at a place like this. Restaurants, and especially kitchens, are like my second home. I've spent a lot of time in them. In fact, it was at a Michelin-starred place in Melbourne where I learned how to cook. The chef there was really friendly and would teach me everything in the kitchen during breaks and downtime. I learned a lot there, amongst the pans and the flames and the yelling chefs. That's where my passion for cooking came from. That's why I would like to open a bakery shop.

Dominika ushers me into a side office at the back. The room is full of documents and files, with one very old computer sitting on the desk. She sits behind the desk and gestures for me to sit in the other chair. I do so, gripping my hands together so that they don't shake.

I'm so goddamn nervous. Quit your shaking, Bay.

It's only because I know how important this job is that I'm so riled up. I know how vital it is I get this waitressing position. I need the money. Fisher, Davy, and Pearl need the money.

"Have you dined here before, Bay?" Dominika asks.

"No, I haven't. I'm new in town."

"Oh," Dominika leans back in her chair and stares at me with her pale blue eyes. She has a penetrating gaze that seems to beam right through me. I shift, uncomfortable and anxious, in my seat. "Well, let me introduce this place to you. We've been around for a few years. We're owned by the Finn family. Do you know them?" she asks.

I shake my head.

The Finn family? The way she says their name makes them sound like a Mafia gang.

"They're a rich and very famous family in New Water. One of them owns the restaurant properly, Cliff Finn."

"Right."

Haven't heard of him.

"Cliff thinks he's in charge, but I have him - what's the

English phrase - *by the balls*. He may be rich, but in here he answers to me."

I laugh and Dominika warmly smiles.

I like her.

"Do you have your resume?" she asks. I hastily nod and pull out my papers from my bag and slide them across the desk. Dominika quickly darts her eyes over them, then back up to me, barely reading my credentials. "Tell me about yourself."

Don't screw this up, Bay.

"Um," I reply, my lips dry. I'm so *freakin'* nervous. "I'm twenty-seven and, as I've said, I'm new to New Water."

"Interesting. Past experiences?"

"I've done a variety of jobs, mainly waitressing, around the country for the last ten years or so."

"Bouncing around, I get it. I've done my fair share of that."

"Yeah, just working in lots of different restaurants."

"Good, good. So, why did you move to New Water?"

"Fisher - my brother - his wife... passed away recently and I've come here to help him and his family. I had no ties anywhere else. New start and all that."

Dominika leans forward and shakes her head. "I'm sorry for your loss."

She's sincere. I really like her. I can sense her warmth and kindness already; it's just a nice vibe she's giving off. "Thanks."

"Tell me more about yourself. Your passions?"

"Oh, I *love* food, especially cooking. That's my passion. I just love to cook."

Dominika laughs. "That's good. I'm the chef around here, as well as the manager. *And* a waitress. I basically do everything. We're going through a big of a rough patch, as you could see by how we have no one dining with us tonight."

I nod, trying not to make it seem like I'm not too judgmental about Rockpool's lack of customers.

"I really need this job," I blurt out. "Like, *really* need it. I'll do anything, pay me whatever, I just need a job."

Woah, where did that come from?

Why did I ramble that out? What was I thinking?

I was practically *begging*.

Dominika doesn't react to my random pleading outburst. She picks up my papers and shuffles them absentmindedly, thinking.

Knock, knock.

Someone's tapping on the door behind us. Dominika left it open when we entered the office, so the knocking is clearly more for show than to be let inside.

"Is the interview going well?" A voice says from the doorway behind me. Dominika looks up, but I can't see who it is without turning completely around in my seat.

It's a male voice. Deep and resonate. Strong.

"Cliff," Dominika replies to the voice with a raise of her eyebrows. "What are you doing in here without a top on?"

"I've just come from a very good swim at the beach and thought I'll swing by and see how things are going?"

"You can't come into this restaurant half-naked, Cliff. It's not right."

"It is my restaurant, though, isn't it?"

"Yeah, but..."

"So, I get to choose what the rules are."

"Put a shirt on, you stupid man." They're teasing each other like old friends and not like this employee-employer thing they seem to have.

"Oh, I don't like your attitude, Dominika. It's my place and I can wear or not wear whatever I want inside it."

Ah.

Cliff.

The man behind me must be Cliff Finn.

The member of the rich and famous family and the owner of the restaurant that Dominika was talking about. That Cliff Finn.

And he's come in without a shirt on?

A little bit arrogant, but okay.

Dominika shakes her head with another smile. "Shut up and come in here, Cliff. Let me introduce you two," she says, fixating her pale blue eyes back on me. "This is Cliff Finn, the owner of Rockpool. Cliff, this is Bay Dover, an applicant to be a waitress here."

I turn in my seat to get a look at this mysterious and all-powerful Cliff Finn.

It's true, he's half-naked. His top is off and he's wet. The first thing I see is his rippling muscles. The man really takes care of himself. There's a prominent six-pack of abs right at my eyeline.

But then I turn my attention to his face. Our eyes meet, and I immediately recognize him.

No freaking way.

It's him.

His eyes widen as he recognizes me as well. An expression of anger and surprise rock his face, probably the same expression as mine.

It's the man from the bank.

Cliff Finn is freaking *Superman*.

Oh, shit.

7

CLIFF

No. Fucking. Way.

Bay Dover?

The girl from the bank? The one who publicly humiliated me?

She's the one getting interviewed at my restaurant. She's the woman sitting right in front of me right now? I didn't think I would ever see her again but, here she is, sitting in my manager's office. Sitting in *my* chair.

The water-throwing chick. She's here.

Looking at her, I know it's one hundred percent her. The brown hair. The pale skin. The large green eyes staring right back at me in shock and horror. It's her alright, I'd recognize her anywhere. It's her, and she's sitting in front of me.

For a second I don't even react; I'm so surprised by what I see.

I really didn't think I'd see that annoying girl ever again.

But the initial shock wears off and both this Bay Dover and I speak at exactly the same time.

"*You?*" We both utter the same word together.

I shake my head and Bay scrunches up her face, narrowing her eyes at me. I see she's taking me all in as well. We're sizing each other up like vicious lions circling before a fight.

I lean against the doorframe of the manager's office, my body going into rigor mortis just by looking at her.

I suddenly feel very exposed that I've walked in here wearing nothing but my shorts. To be honest, I didn't think I'll be running into the demon girl of my nightmares when I strolled in here a few moments ago, and now I'm suddenly very aware of how my torso is very exposed to this chick. My naked chest is right above her.

And she's clearly trying hard not to check me out.

Can't blame her. I do work out. Hard.

"What are you doing here?" I whisper to her. I try to sound menacing, but my voice comes out wavering. I'm still in shock.

Man up, Cliff. Get over the fact this chick's here and stomp her pretty ass.

"An... interview," the glass-chucking chick stammers in response.

She's as shocked as I am. Good.

This is my restaurant.

My domain. I'm in control here.

"Get out," I reply, my fists clenching. I take one step into the office and away from the doorframe. "Before I punish you for what you did this morning."

The girl seems unfazed by my comment. In fact, she seems renewed by it. Her hesitant expression disappears, replaced by a steely focus in her eyes. Shit. "Is that a threat?" she asks.

She's calling my bluff.

"Wait, you two know each other?" Dominika asks from behind the desk. She has no clue what's going on.

"Kinda," Bay answers quickly.

"We met today," I reply to my restaurant manager.

"If I remember correctly, you pushed past me into the bank and then you made a scene," the fiery brown-head bluntly says at me like she's throwing javelins.

Oh, you want a fight?

I can give you a fight.

"Actually, if I remember correctly, you were the one who made a scene. Do you even remember the glass of water? What you did in front of everyone?"

"I did that only because you were being a colossal dick. You deserved that."

"I recall you were taking your sweet-ass time, so you needed some encouragement to get the hell outta there. You were holding up the line."

"Screw you," she replies. "You were rude and impolite. Have you ever heard of patience?"

"No, I haven't," I say. "Mentioning it, I'm pretty impatient now for you to get out of my restaurant. Go now."

"Are you kicking me out?"

"Don't make me force you," I reply. "I could pick you up right now and throw you out myself."

Yeah, I bet she'll fight back as I do so. I'm itching for it.

"Hold on one second," Dominika interrupts me. "I haven't finished my interview."

"The interview's over, Dominika," I reply. "Bay - or whatever your name is - you're leaving. Get out."

Dominika raises her hand, and I growl back at her. I don't have time for her silly attitude right now, but I've got to respect her. Without Dominika, I have nothing. Without her, Rockpool would already be shut down and I'll be deemed a failure by both my family and the entire town of New Water. I need this crazy European chef, and she knows that.

Oh, she knows it.

Despite me owning the place, she has power over me. And she knows how to wield that power.

Damn.

I do like her.

And now I just *have* to listen to whatever she's going to say.

"The interview is not over until I say it's over," Dominika replies with that smug gleam in her eyes I know too well. She never passes up an opportunity to assert her dominance over me.

"Dominika," I say, nodding out of the doorway. "Can we talk in the kitchen?"

"Now?"

"Yes."

"With or without Bay?"

I scowl at my restaurant manager. I really don't have time for her cheeky games.

"What do you think?"

"Sure, I'll come outside."

I glare at Bay sitting in the chair directly in front of me. "You sit right there and don't touch anything. You'll be leaving in a moment, so don't get too comfortable."

Bay shrugs back. "Well, this is, by far, the weirdest interview I've ever been in."

"Excuse me for a moment, Bay." Dominika stands and follows me out of the manager's office. I catch her giving a sweet smile to Bay just as she leaves.

What is this? Girl power? Gang up on Cliff day?

I storm into the kitchen, making it obvious to Dominika how angry I'm feeling. She struts in behind me, taking her sweet-ass time to follow like she's twisting the dagger into my restraint. We stand by the pots and pans, me with my arms crossed and Dominika flicking her long blonde hair back over her shoulder nonchalantly.

"Kick her out," I command. "Now."

"No."

"Throw her out of my restaurant."

"No."

"She's not welcome here."

"She is," Dominika replies, her hard European face unflinching. A wall. "I'm actually thinking of hiring her."

I splutter. "What?"

"You heard me."

"No way are we to have her on staff."

"Why not? What happened between you two? Tell me what's got you so riled up."

"She chucked a glass of water over me."

Dominika laughs, covering her mouth with her hand. "That's it?"

"She *did* it in public. She humiliated me."

"She called you a dick in there. Were you acting like a dick? Is that why she did that?"

"No." I'm incredulous.

"Be truthful."

"No."

"*Really?* I know you, Cliff. You can be a right ass sometimes."

"So, you're actually thinking of hiring this girl who publicly humiliated me? I'm your boss."

"Yes, I think I will," Dominika replies. "I *like* her, Cliff. She's good, she has lots of restaurant experience, and she'll work for cheap. We need that right now, and you know it. We've practically lost every member of staff except for me, and I don't know if you've read any of our recent financial records, but we're *in the shit*. We're gonna close very soon unless we get help."

"Help?"

"You can always turn to your family."

"No. Never."

"Fine, then. Fair enough. That just means we need to hire staff. Staff who will work for cheap. Staff like Bay here."

I may come from a family of billionaires, but I am *not* going to use my family's money to prop up this business. I want to prove to them I can do this on my own, without my family's wealth. Throwing my family's money at this problem would be like playing a video game on *easy* mode.

I don't want that reputation within my own family.

"And you think this Bay Dover is the help we need?"

"Yes."

"No way. I'm stopping this now. You can't hire her."

Dominika sighs like she's dealing with a toddler's temper tantrum. She raises her eyebrows at me. "When you hired me, we agreed I had power over hiring and firing decisions, and this clearly falls within my jurisdiction. I have power here, as you promised me. I'm hiring her, Cliff, and there's nothing you can do about it."

"And what if I fire you?"

Dominika laughs again. She leans up on her toes and gives me a peck on the cheek. "You'll never dare fire me, sweetie. I'm the one keeping this place together and you know it," she whispers. Despite my hollow threats, I know she's right. And she knows I know. Dominika turns and sashays back into the manager's office, calling out behind her. "The girl's hired. She starts tomorrow."

Fucking hell.

That European woman's gonna be the death of me.

And now she's gonna hire Bay Dover. At my restaurant.
This is unbelievable. An outrage.
Do I have no say in this?
Bay Dover working at my business?
That girl, she's got a whole lot coming to her.

8

BAY

"Okay, what's five minus one?"

Pearl's little face scrunches up as she thinks really hard for an answer to my question. I try to remain silent and not laugh. I try to not betray how cute I think she is knowing that it'll only annoy her and will probably mean the end of this good flow we've gotten into her homework. We're *so* close to finishing for the day and I don't want it to end in tears.

She pokes her tongue out and opens her eyes, excited to come up with an answer. "Four!"

Her happy little face is so kissable; I want to peck it all over, but I hold back.

"Great work. So, if that's five minus one, then what is five minus two?"

This one stumps her. She bites her lip and frowns. I lean forward from behind her and write out a series of numbers.

1 2 3 4 5.

I point to them each in turn with my pencil, letting Pearl count them out one by one.

"One, two, um... three, four, and that's five!"

"So, if we take away two from five, what number is this one?"

"Oh, *three!*"

"Correct!"

"Can I have a cookie now?"

"Alright, then. Only because you've been a good girl."

Okay. Fine. I am also *bribing* Pearl to do her homework with the promise of her favorite food. Chocolate-chip cookies. But we are making amazing progress, so you can't really fault my methods, corrupt as they are.

I lean back in my seat as I watch Pearl race around to the kitchen cabinet and reach up on her tippy toes to impatiently grab the cookie jar, super excited to get her number one treat.

Yep, my brother has one hell of a cute daughter.

As I watch her struggle to open the cookie jar, my mind casts back to last night, and that strange interview.

I never expected to see Cliff there. I never expected to run back into the man I humiliated with a glass of water. I certainly didn't expect him to be the *owner* of the place I was trying to get a job at, the one place in town that would be accepting of my limited skill set.

I didn't expect Dominika to come waltzing back into the manager's office offering me the waitressing job after her talk with Cliff in the kitchen, which I tried, and failed, to overhear.

I didn't expect to immediately accept the job as soon as she offered it to me.

Hey, I need the money.

And it seems like Rockpool needs a waitress.

"That's enough homework for today," I say to my niece

as I watch her greedily bite into the cookie she's taken from the jar. Pearl's little face beams up with the thoughts of the next hour taken up by cartoons and dolls. I let her get away with too much, but I can't resist her cute face and singsong voice. I'm not the best auntie in the world *for nothing*.

"You going to watch TV with me?" she asks, finishing the giant cookie in about two eager bites.

"Unfortunately not, sweetie. I have to get ready."

"Get ready for what?"

I grab her in a cuddle and kiss her tiny forehead. "I have to get ready for work, Pearl. Today's my first day."

"Your first day?"

"Yeah, it's like my first day of school. You remember that?"

"Are you nervous? I was nervous on my first day of school, but then I made lots and lots of friends and now they're all invited to my birthday party."

"Your birthday's not for another three months, Pearl. There's no need to hand out invitations just yet. But, yes, I'm a little bit nervous about today. My boss is a scary man."

"Oh, no. Is he a monster?"

I chuckle. "Yes, a scary monster but, don't worry, I know how to deal with him. He thinks he's scary, but inside he's just a big old scaredy-cat."

I mimic a scary monster, turning my fingers into talons and letting out a mighty roar. Pearl giggles at my display and runs to the living room. I follow her in and help her turn on the TV to her favorite cartoon. My niece sits back on the sofa and watches the screen with her big button eyes, sucking her thumb.

I can't avoid glancing at the photo frame above the TV. In the photo are Fisher and his wife, arms tightly wrapped around each other in front of the skyline of New York City. It was taken the day he proposed to her. That first spark I remember seeing they had together, right on through their wedding, that spark was what gave birth to my beautiful niece and nephew. They continued that spark even through her cancer diagnosis, right on to the end. Their love never faltered. Not once.

What they had was true love.

And I know I will never find something like that, not when Fisher and his wife set such a perfect standard. Their love was something *rare*, something I know I can never experience.

It really was true love.

* * *

"Alright, let me do this quickly so I don't have to see your annoying face any longer than I should, Bay Dover."

Wow. What a wonderful start to my first shift this is turning out to be.

Cliff Finn motions at me to join him by the computer terminal in the restaurant bar.

"This is the till system. I'm not going to spend my time going through it with you, so I expect you to play around with it yourself and learn it on your own. Understood?"

I salute mockingly. "Yes, *sir*."

Cliff rolls his eyes at my sarcastic gesture.

I can't believe Cliff Finn is the one training me.

Why can't it be Dominika?

"I need you to be taking this seriously," he says.

"I would be if you weren't being an unserious teacher," I reply.

"Well, I might as well just leave you to figure everything on your own if you're going to have an attitude."

An attitude? He's been the one grumbling since I started.

I got to the restaurant this evening expecting Dominika to be taking me around and showing me the place, instead, I found out she was busy in the kitchen cooking up the food for the few customers we had in the place and that my training would have to be taken over by Cliff, despite his many, many protestations.

He really didn't want to be doing this.

And I really don't want him to be training me.

But here we are.

The restaurant is a little busy, but nowhere near full. Saturday night and there are only a few tables. Insane. The only workers in here are Dominika and me. And Cliff, if you counted him.

If he actually does any work beyond endlessly complaining about me.

I flick my hair back as Cliff takes me towards the front. "Well, I think I can safely say this is, hands down, the worst induction I've ever had the pleasure of going through. It's only superseded by that insane interview I had with you barging in on yesterday."

"Well, I'm only doing this because Dominika's busy in the kitchen, so it's pretty shit for me, too. I don't want to be teaching your sorry ass. It's the last thing I want. Or need."

"Excuse me?"

Cliff ignores me and waves his hand towards the staircase. "Toilets are down the stairs, and I am expecting you to clean them at the end of every night. No moaning."

"Sounds like fun."

We reach the front doors. Cliff takes a menu off the pile on the reception counter and thrusts it into my hands. "Read this and memorize it," he commands. "I want you to be able to list out every item we have by the end of next week. You got that?"

I'm about to open my mouth in protest, but I'm cut off

by the front door of the restaurant. It swings open with a creak.

Customers?

A group of adults walks in. Four of them. Two guys and two women.

Before I can comprehend what's going on, one of the men rushes forward and tackles Cliff. I take a step back in horror, but quickly realize he's being friendly when I notice Cliff laughing. He pushes the guy away, patting him on the back.

Right. They know each other.

"Cove," my boss says with a wide smile. "Good to see you."

The man who Cliff pushed away - Cove - looks around the restaurant in wonder. "Man, you said this place wasn't busy, but I didn't expect to see it this quiet."

"That's because you're here," the other man says. I can't help but notice he's wearing a *very* nice suit. His accent is like a weird hybrid of Australian and cut-glass English. I got to admit it's *very* sexy. "You're scaring away all his customers."

Cove jokingly lifts up a fist. "Shut up, Skipper, or I'll knock you out."

"You can't knock out a fly," Cliff laughs, and Cove swerves to tackle him again, arms wrapped around Cliff's waist.

The two men are tall and handsome, just like Cliff. The two women in the group, presumably their girlfriends or partners, follow behind. The men are play-fighting and ripping each other whilst their partners roll their eyes at each other. I bet this is a typical display of masculine dominance in their household.

One of them, a pretty brown-haired girl that looks like Natalie Portman, turns and sighs at me with a smile on her face. "If you're wondering if they're always like this," she says in an American accent. "Then I can answer *yes*. They're always like this."

The other girl winks at me. "They're even worse at home. They're like wild animals when not in public," she says before turning to the wrestlers. "Come along, boys. Let's not cause a scene, let's go to our table. Maybe I'll let you draw with the kids' crayons if you all behave."

"Alright, Sandy," the suited half-English guy replies sarcastically, fixing his collar ruffled from the play-fight.

The group heads into the restaurant and to a corner booth at the back, leaving Cliff and me alone at the front door.

"You know them?" I ask my boss.

"Cove and Sandy are my cousins, and Ripley and Skipper are their spouses. They're the closest thing I have to family."

"Oh, right."

I squint towards the group. Cove does look like Cliff. Both are super broad-shouldered and tall. Athletic is the word.

Throughout the rest of the next hour, I pass by their table plenty of times as I get used to the layout of the restaurant. I get to overhear their conversation as I pass by. Yeah, I'm snooping, but I'm curious about Cliff's family. The girls seem super friendly and the guys are super charismatic, so I simply just have to find out more about them.

Cliff dodges around the bar to make cocktails for them.

"Go and take their order," he hisses at me as he dumps a load of ice into a cocktail shaker.

I'm pretty nervous. I don't want to screw up the table of my boss' family, not on my first shift, but I also don't want to give Cliff the satisfaction of seeing me upset and anxious, so

I hold my head up high and march towards their booth, fetching around in my apron for my notepad and pen.

Before I reach their table, I can overhear their conversation already.

"Did you know she's just been announced as the new star of the *Vindicator Team*?" the American girl asks the group, leaning in conspiratorially.

Cove grabs her arm. "The movie series? The superhero one?"

"Yeah, duh. The one that Sandy and I love."

The other guy - Skipper - nods. "Yeah, you guys never shut up about it."

"And *she's* the new star in it? I thought she was a supermodel."

"Well, now she's an actress."

"Can you believe that Cliff dated a supermodel who's now about to become one of the biggest acting stars on the planet?"

Cliff? Dating? A superstar?

He's dated a model that now is in the box-office-smashing movie franchise? I wonder who dumped who?

I'm still thinking about it all when I reach their table. I'm still daydreaming about Cliff dating a supermodel when I ask them for their order. "Know what you want, guys?"

I'm still caught up in thinking about Cliff and this now-famous actress when the group quickly reels off their choices and I hastily write them down, in shorthand, on my notepad.

I head back to the bar and input their orders onto the till machine.

"You're taking your time," Cliff says, peeking over my shoulder as I tap methodically away at the screen. The order digitally shoots through to the kitchen, to be printed out for Dominika to make.

"Well, maybe if you taught me how this system works, then *maybe* I might be at a pace closer to your liking," I reply to the annoying hunk, and Cliff grunts in response. He sulks away to his family's table, carrying a tray of the cocktails he's made. They all cheer him as he flourishes them onto the table in front of them.

I serve the other customers in the restaurant until Dominika rings the bell for the Finn family's order. I head towards the kitchen, but Cliff raises a hand at me, gesturing that he wants to take the food out himself.

Sure, you do it, pal.

I watch from the bar as he takes the plates, balancing three at a time on his arms, from the kitchen. I watch as he asks around who has what plate.

I watch on as there's a lot of shaking of heads and Cliff looking confused.

Someone says something, and Cliff's head lifts up and turns to me. He glares at me with a look just like the one he gave me in the bank the other day.

And I instantly know what's up. Why the shaking heads. Why Cliff's glare.

My hands clutch the side of the bar.

Shit, I've gotten his family's order wrong.

9

BAY

OH NO, *oh no, oh no.*

I've messed up their order.

I'd been daydreaming too much about Cliff and his supermodel ex-girlfriend and what they were talking about, that I completely screwed up what his family had ordered.

I can see in Cliff's eyes - the way he stares me down across the restaurant like he has lasers - that I have really *royally* screwed up this time.

Big time.

Fuck.

With a flick of his head, his hands full of steaming plates, he motions me to the kitchen. I let go of the counter of the bar and follow him to the back, my breathing heavy. I've really, really screwed up. My first day and I barely make it an hour into my shift.

Typical me.

I pass by the table full of his family members, and I murmur out a quick *sorry* as I skip pass, but before I can disappear into the kitchen, the blonde girl - Cliff's cousin, I think - grabs me by the wrist. She holds me tightly, not letting me go.

"Don't worry about Cliff," she whispers to me so that the others on the table can't hear. "He can be a real dick to everyone when he's in a funk, including his own cousins."

"I really am sorry about what's happened."

"Honestly, don't worry about it. And don't let Cliff get to you. I'll sort him out. Don't worry about it."

"Yeah?"

"I'll have a word with him. If he yells at you, then he's in the wrong. He can be a right prick sometimes."

I nod slowly and she lets me go with a faint smile. I avert my eyes from hers, embarrassed. I don't want strangers feeling pity for me.

Why did I even accept this job in the first place?

Because I need the money, duh.

I really do need the money.

I hesitantly walk towards the kitchen, the words of Cliff's blonde cousin echoing in my mind.

Don't let him get to you.

Oh, I won't.

But this was my mistake. I screwed up here, but I won't back down from a fight with Cliff if he's so pissed at me.

I open the doors of the kitchen, the smell of cooking food wafting over me, and storm towards Cliff. He's standing next to Dominika, his hands still full of the mistake plates. Seeing me, his face turns as red as the cooking stove.

"What on earth was that?" he asks, a spit of venom in his voice. "You've completely fucked up the order."

He's a pretty shit Gordon Ramsay.

"I didn't mean to."

"Doesn't matter if you meant to or not, you still did it."

"Yeah, I made a mistake, but it's my first day. Cut me

some slack. I can go out there and apologize and tell them it was my fault if you want."

Cliff closes his eyes like he's trying to hold himself back. "You know how much you've embarrassed me today?" he asks rhetorically in a quiet, slow voice full of threat. "You know how much you've humiliated me in front of my own family? This is who you are, Bay. You threw water over me in public and now you've humiliated me in front of my cousins. It's the end of the line for you."

Dominika steps in front of the man. "Listen to her, Cliff. It's her first day. If she did anything wrong, it's the mistake of the teacher, not the student."

"You hired her, and now she's screwed up. Can you see why I was against all of this?"

"It's her first day, so I guess she screwed up because of her teacher." Dominika raises an eyebrow at Cliff. "And who was her teacher?"

Cliff grunts in response and storms past me and out of the kitchen. He points back at me and shouts back before the kitchen doors close. "You need to work this out, Bay, or you're *fired*, you get me?"

The door slams close and it's like wind's been knocked out of me with Cliff's sudden departure. I lose my balance and stumble to the kitchen counter, grasping it with both hands to steady myself. Dominika strolls toward me and places her hand reassuringly on my shoulder.

"Don't worry about the dickhead," she says.

"How can I not when he shouts at me like that?"

"Back in my hometown in Poland, we have a saying. *Drink and forget the bastard*. It's more about dealing with your ex-boyfriend, but I think it's pretty applicable in these circumstances."

Dominika leans down below the counter and I tilt my

head to see what she's doing. She reemerges a moment later, holding a bottle of white wine.

I gasp at her sneakiness. "Where did that come from?" I ask.

She raises a finger to her lips and hushes me.

"Keep this as our little secret, just between us," she says. "This is a way I get through a shift when Cliff's being a little dick."

She offers me the bottle, nodding to me to drink it. I do so. The wine is nice. Strong. Refreshing.

I guess it's a good idea to keep a secret stash when you have to work with Cliff.

"Good, huh?"

"Yeah," I reply. "It's very good. Thanks."

Dominika takes the bottle from me and has her own sip. "He's not always like this," she explains. "He's just very stressed at the moment."

"Right."

"You know he really likes you, right?"

My eyes widen and I shake my head. *Likes me?* "What are you, Dominika? Insane? Of course, he doesn't like me."

"Oh, he does. I know him very well, so I know when he likes someone."

"What?"

"He likes you."

"Well, if he does like me, then he has a very strange way of showing it."

"Cliff's had a bad few months."

I lean against the kitchen counter, no longer feeling dizzy. "Is this about his ex?"

Dominika perks up at the mention of his supermodel ex-girlfriend. "How do you know about that?"

"I overheard his cousins talking about her, about how she was a supermodel and is now going to be a big famous

actress or something. Do you know anything about her?"
I ask.

Maybe Dominika can tell me more about Cliff's love life. It sounds interesting.

She laughs. "He's very private about that kind of stuff. You probably know more than I do about it now."

"Right."

She hands me the bottle and I take another long gulp of the fine liquid.

So.

He's had a supermodel girlfriend. And she might've dumped him. No wonder he's in such an aggressive and rude mood, he's probably devastated. Still trying to get over his failed relationship.

I can't relate. I've never had a boyfriend. I've never even been on a proper date before, just a few drunken one-night stands that never led anywhere.

I suspect Cliff's probably ripped up inside over his ex.

So, there's probably more to Cliff Finn than meets the eye.

Maybe I was too quick to judge him.

Or maybe I should just quit now. Maybe he *is* a total dick, and I should get out now before he goes crazy on me. There's enough red flags here to tell me so.

But what Dominika said to me still rings in my ear.

He likes you.

10

CLIFF

I OPEN the front door of Rockpool and feel the cool nighttime air softly brush my cheek.

It's late. The main street of New Water is quiet; it's always eerie this time of night. The only sounds are the crashing of waves on the shore just around the corner. The sounds of any typical Australian small town.

I turn and lock the restaurant door behind me. Inside, Rockpool is dark. Silent. Even more empty than it was tonight with customers, and that's saying something.

I take the keys out the door and test the handle.

Yeah, it's locked.

I think back on tonight, and on Bay and her fucking up of my cousins' order. I do feel a little bit guilty for the rageful reaction I had back there in the kitchen, but she did screw up big time. She did embarrass me in front of my family. Thinking about it even now makes my blood boil.

How dare she insult me like that literally a day after the whole water glass incident?

I bet it was all on purpose.

She definitely would do something like that to irritate me. She knew they were my family, so she was probably bursting at the chance to humiliate me then as well.

I can't believe Dominika really hired her. I bet she did it to spite me. She loves to infuriate me like that.

But Bay? She's crossed the line tonight. Her first shift and she screwed up majorly.

Right, that's it. I'm going to fire her.

I'll do it tomorrow. Screw Dominika and her attitude; I'm going to get rid of Bay Dover and there's nothing my chef can do about it. I can't have this girl ruining my already-failing business.

Even if she is so pretty.

Even if she makes my stomach turn every time I see her.

That's the one thing I'm trying to keep under wraps, from everyone and especially from myself, the fact that I may actually quite like this girl.

Fuck.

I may actually like Bay Dover.

She's got sass and is unafraid to talk back at me. Being from one of the richest families in the country means that barely anyone has ever done that to me, and I *kinda like it.* She doesn't give a fuck who I am or what my last name means. She thinks I'm a dick, and she's unafraid to point it out.

Maybe that's why I am acting like so much of a dick to her. Maybe I am overcompensating because of my true feelings for her. I'm overdoing my aggressive attitude towards her simply because I don't want anyone, especially Bay herself, to realize I might have *feelings* for her.

Ugh.

I've promised myself not to get tangled up with another girl so soon after Cleo. No way. I can't have my heart ripped out like that again. I don't ever want to experience that again. *No, sir.*

And Bay, with her sass and her confidence and her *fucking* beautiful face, screams danger to me.

I need to back off from her.

And that's why I intend to fire her gorgeous ass at the earliest chance. Tomorrow.

I can't deal with *feelings* again. Not for a girl, and not for someone as bad for me as Bay Dover.

It'll be like what happened with Cleo, repeated.

I stuff the restaurant keys into my pocket and take in a deep breath of the night air, letting it fill my lungs.

Yeah, I'll fire her tomorrow.

I step down to the sidewalk and head towards my car.

Parked next to my vehicle is another car I recognize.

Shit.

And leaning against it is someone I recognize equally well.

Double shit.

Sandy.

My cousin.

She's leaning against her car that's parked right next to mine, her arms crossed, glaring at me as I approach.

"Hello, Cliff," she says, her blonde hair gently swaying in the cool night air.

"Hi, Sandy."

"Nice night," she replies.

"What are you doing here, and so late?" I ask. "Don't you have school tomorrow?"

"My students can wait," she replies. "First, I have to deal with you."

"Right, so you're annoyed about your food order? I can refund you if you like."

Sandy doesn't react to my little joke.

"I'm talking about that waitress," she says.

Fuck. Of course.

Even though she isn't here, Bay Dover can still find ways to fuck me over.

I definitely need to fire her ass.

"What waitress?"

Sandy is unamused. Her frown deepens. She's not a good person to tease. I should know, I've been on the back end of her lectures more times than I can count. She's good at those, probably comes from her training as a teacher. She thinks she knows how to handle difficult boys like me.

Well, I'm not your usual naughty schoolkid, Sandy. I can bite too.

"You know who I'm talking about," she replies sternly. "I was watching her today. She's a good girl."

"Really? That's your expert opinion, is it?"

"She's too good for you, Cliff."

"She should be thanking me for a job, not screwing up my restaurant orders."

"Listen to me, Cliff."

I sigh and thrust my hands into my pockets, meeting my cousin's glare. "Alright, I'm listening. Say what you have to say."

"Take this seriously."

There's a pause, and I realize she's waiting for me to answer her.

She's really using her teaching skills now, isn't she? She's really pulling out her stern teacher voice.

"Okay, I will take this seriously."

"Don't screw her around, okay? Don't hurt her."

"I won't."

Sandy raises her eyebrows. "Promise me, Cliff. She's a good girl. She doesn't deserve your dick behavior."

I sigh again. "Sure," I reply.

"I'll be watching."

"Okay."

She really knows how to attack me, doesn't she?

Sandy smiles and nods. "Good, then."

"Alright."

She continues watching me.

"Good."

"Okay, so can I get to my car now, or do I have to get on my knees and beg for that, too?"

Sandy exhales a deep breath. "I know what's wrong," she says slowly.

I don't like the way she looks at me now.

"What? What do you mean, *you know what's wrong*?"

"You're still hurting."

I laugh at her comment. "Hurting?"

Ridiculous.

"Yeah. I know it's all to do with Cleo. You're still hurting from what she did to you. I get it. You can talk to me about it if you'd like."

I roll my eyes. "Get lost," I reply.

"Fine, deny it. I know when someone's heartbroken, though. I've been through it myself."

"Shut up," I reply, taking out my car keys and unlocking my car. "I don't have time for this pseudo-therapy. I'm going home, and you better get some sleep before school in the morning."

Sandy raises her hands in the air in mock surrender. "I'm just saying," she says. "I know what's wrong. There's nothing bad for you to admit that your heart is broken."

"See you around, cousin."

I jump into my Lamborghini, shutting the door so that I don't have to deal with Sandy anymore. I peek at her through my rearview mirror. She's still leaning on her car, staring at me.

What is it with the women in my life today? First Dominika and now Sandy? Let alone that Bay Dover.

But maybe Sandy is right. I shouldn't fire the new girl. That'll be a real asshole move to do. I may be shallow, but I'm not that bad.

I'll give her a few days' trial. See how she does. I can always fire her pretty face later.

Sandy thinks I'm heartbroken over Cleo.

I scoff in my car and ignite the engine.

Heartbroken. As if.

But, deep down, I know it to be true.

Sandy's right.

Even though I put on an uncaring mask, I'm only trying to hide the fact that Cleo broke my heart and that I've still got to mend it. I'm still feeling the pain.

But I can do this on my own, alright? I don't need some women like Sandy and Dominika to act like amateur psychologists for me. I'm a man; I can deal with my feelings on my own, thank you very much.

I don't need their help.

I don't need Bay's help.

I can manage on my own.

Fuck Cleo. Fuck Sandy.

And, most of all, fuck Bay.

11

TWO MONTHS EARLIER

CLIFF

I CHECK myself out in the hotel mirror. My body is *perfect*. Years of working out - hard - have toned my body into one hell of a sculpture. My thick, hard abs are visibly popping out, and you can trace your finger around the edges of my solid pecs. My jawline is sharp and defined. My short designer stubble is immaculate.

I look like a Greek God.

Oh, yes. I do.

I admire my body as I pull my shirt over my shoulders and I wink at myself in the mirror.

Handsome devil, you.

Satisfied, I turn and stroll away from the hotel mirror and towards the balcony. Of course, I've booked out the most expensive and best suite in the luxury hotel. Nothing lower would do for me. I deserve the *very* best.

Some may call me cocky or arrogant, but I prefer the term *cultured*. Like my body, I don't put up with anything below perfection.

Standing on the balcony, I take in the foreign air and look down at the famous city below me, at all the buildings lit up below my hotel suite.

Paris.

City of lights.

City of love.

I've been here for a few weeks. For the past few years, I've been traveling through Europe. Partying. Fucking. Just like the kings of old, Europe's been my domain, and I'm doing what any self-respecting twenty-something-year-old drop-dead *gorgeous* bachelor with tons of money to spare should do. I've been traveling, clubbing, and fucking hot women.

But now I want to settle down.

I've had my fill of booze and women, and it does help that I've found a girl who's a keeper. A girl who's perfect for me, both in looks and *class*.

Cleo Dash.

I've been dating the American supermodel for nearly a year now, and everything's been going *perfectly*. We're the perfect match. We're both incredibly good-looking, rich, successful, and young. We have it all. Anyone would agree we're the perfect match.

I scan my eyes over the Parisian skyline. The Eiffel Tower sits alone in the distance, in full view of my hotel suite balcony. It's lit up in a golden haze.

Damn right, Paris is one of my favorite cities.

Ring.

The doorbell chimes. I head back inside from the balcony, away from the city lights, and open the hotel door. A waiter with a trolley is waiting for me. On top of the trolley is an ice bucket, and inside is a bottle of the finest Champagne money can buy.

Champagne in a Paris hotel room. Perfect.

"Come this way," I instruct the waiter, guiding him to the center of the large hotel suite just in front of the balcony. I quickly tip him and usher him to leave. I inspect the Champagne and the glasses for any speck of dust or any blemishes. None. Great.

I check the time on my watch. Late evening.

She should be arriving at any moment.

I dash to my suitcase by the king-sized bed and pull out a small box. I double-check its contents.

A diamond engagement ring. One of the best I've ever seen, and it is mine. Mine to give out.

You see, I'm planning to propose to my girlfriend tonight.

I want us to get engaged.

I want her to be my wife.

Giddy with excitement, I go and wait by the champagne. I stare out across to the Eiffel Tower; you can see it from the room. Out of all the cities to propose in, Paris is the best, the one I dreamed about proposing in when I was younger. And now I'm here with a ring in my pocket, ready to propose to the girlfriend of my dreams.

I hear the unlocking of the hotel door and I ready myself.

Just on time.

The door opens and in walks Cleo Dash. She really does look like a supermodel. She doesn't look bad under any light or from any angle. It's like she's an angel. Long blonde hair. Angular face. Full lips. Slim body. She's *perfect* in the looks department.

Just like me.

"Hey, babe," I say as she steps into the room. She's

wearing a designer dress, low cut at the cleavage and sparkling under the hotel lights. She's just been out at a long dinner with some of her girlfriends, the perfect opportunity for me to get the room ready for my proposal.

"Hi," she replies in her soft American accent. As a supermodel, Cleo has worked for all the major fashion houses in Europe. Like me, she's also a bit of a nomad. We both flitter around the capital cities of Europe in their luxury hotels rather than have a specific home. We can afford to do that.

She turns to head to the bathroom, but I call out before she can move. "I need to show you something, Cleo."

"What is it, darling?"

"Stay," I reply, gesturing her over. "I need to show you something."

She eyes the champagne suspiciously as I bring her over to the center of the room; double-checking the Eiffel Tower is in view behind us. I've secretly set up my phone in the corner to take a video of this special occasion. Cleo has millions of followers on her social media, so I just know she'll want to share this proposal with the world after it's done.

Truth be told, I'm pretty proud of this proposal I've put together. It's fitting for both of us, and for our status. One of the best hotel suits in Paris overlooking the Eiffel Tower doesn't get any higher in classiness.

Can't get any better than that.

"What is it?" Cleo asks me.

I don't give her the chance to ask any more questions. Instead, I quickly take a knee in front of her and pull out the ring box.

"Cleo - Miss Dash - since the first time I met you, I was in love..."

"Oh, *babe*."

I'm immediately cut off by Cleo raising a manicured fingernail. Unlike the happy expression I expect, her face is frowning instead.

I blink.

"What?" I ask.

Why is she interrupting?

"Don't keep going," she replies blankly. "Don't do this."

"What do you mean?" I stutter, unable to mask my surprise.

"*Babe*, you don't need to do this."

"What?"

"You don't need to do all this." Cleo gestures around at the Champagne and the ring I am currently offering up to her. "You can stop now, babe."

I can't help but stammer. "I'm *proposing* to you."

"Oh, I can see that, and I'm saying *no*."

What.

My heart stops.

She's saying no?

"I don't believe this."

Cleo starts to laugh. She barely laughs at anything, so it's an unusual sight to see. "This is silly," she says.

"What is?" I'm still on my knee, unable to process what's going on.

"All of this. It's all very silly, babe. It's all very... *sincere*." Cleo laughs again.

"What's so funny? I am sincere. I'm trying to propose."

"You're funny. You're so emotional, babe. Of course, I'm not going to marry you, you're far too emotional for me. All this, the champagne and the ring and the little speech you have prepared, it's all just too earnest. You're such a little boy."

"What?"

"Can't you see our relationship has been something

more of a *mutual benefit* than something deeper? It was all for the Instagram likes, for the celebrity of it. For your family and my modeling career. If you're going to act like this, then I'm not prepared to go any further."

"I don't understand."

"Oh, you thought this was something *deeper*? I get it now. Oh, babe, you're such a *little boy*. I thought you understood what was going on, but it turns out you don't."

She laughs again, turns, and heads towards the hotel door.

"Where are you going?" I ask, blinking again. I'm still unable to comprehend what's happening.

Cleo spins to face me, still laughing. "Oh, this is over, babe. You and me. Us. It's over," she says as she heads out of the suite. "You're just too *much* for me."

And then she was gone.

Cleo Dash walked out on my life.

And that was the last time I saw her. We never spoke again.

And now I read she's going to be the new star of the *Vindicator Team*, no longer just an international supermodel. Now she's going to be the new face of the blockbuster film series?

Great way to rub it in.

I flew back home from Paris the next day after the failed proposal, devastated. I flew back to New Water, to where I was born and raised. Far away from the bright lights of the capital cities of Europe. I needed to lie low and lick my wounds. I took over the management of Rockpool and decided to hide away.

And especially not get seriously involved with another girl again. I seriously can't afford to be hurt like that again. Memories of that Paris hotel room haunt my dreams every night.

So, yeah, Sandy is right to say I'm heartbroken. Anyone would be by the way Cleo treated me.

And I've sworn myself off fancying girls again.

Well, that was until Bay Dover waltzed into my life and threw a glass of water over me.

12

PRESENT DAY

BAY

It's my second day working as a waitress at Rockpool, and things aren't going well.

Not at all.

My problems began when Cliff saw me enter to start my shift, and it only intensifies when a particular group of customers walks through the front door.

One particular customer.

But when I began my shift, I didn't know what was to come today. I came into the restaurant with a smile on my face, ready to start my second day and all prepared to deal with anything Cliff decides to throw at me. I resolved, last night, to put his weird aggressive displays behind me and to give him the benefit of the doubt when it comes to his attitude. He probably is going through a shitty time with whatever happened with his ex, so I might as well be cheery and agreeable and see if he falls into line. See if my positivity rubs off on him.

But clearly, it doesn't.

The moment I walked into the restaurant, Cliff ignores me. He ignores me throughout the entire shift. As I enter the restaurant, I give him a bright *hello* and he grunts in reply. It only goes worse from there. Beyond that initial grunt, he acts like I'm not here.

This is worse than dealing with Davy or any one of his teenage male friends.

Cliff doesn't even seem to acknowledge my existence at all, not even when I put orders through the till system or deliver drinks to tables. He gives me the cold shoulder. Literally.

I'm *so* tempted to make a scene of it, to tell him off or confront him about it. But I don't do that. I don't give him the pleasure of losing my cool. I go into the kitchen and say hello to Dominika, trying my best to suppress my anger at the gorgeous man at the bar who's completely ignoring me.

I instead resolve to stay calm. Collected. Not stir the pot. Pretend everything's okay.

That's sure to annoy him more than if I blow my temper.

I know he wants me to lose my cool, but I'm not going to give him the satisfaction. The muscular hunk will have to stay moping around behind the bar. I won't fight him or his attitude.

Not today.

But it still pisses me off. His behavior still makes me boil inside.

Why can't he just be nice?

That's simple, right? Be nice. That's all I'm asking. It's not much I want, just some basic courtesy.

But he'll still deny me that.

He's so bitter.

Such a sulky man for being so handsome.

Just soak it up, dude.

Take it on your chin, mate.

I don't need his negative energy.

And then the *customer* arrives, and that's when my second shift at Rockpool goes from bad to worse.

* * *

It's a table of six, and they come in through the restaurant door about halfway through the shift. The particular *customer* is the male of the group, the Dad of the family. He leads his family of women through the restaurant door. His wife and four teenage daughters.

"Six," he barks at me.

"Do you have a reservation, sir?" I ask, tapping at the computer terminal to find his booking.

"Six."

It's just another bark from him. I can find him a table anyway, but it would be helpful, if he does have a reservation, to cross his name off the list.

"Have you booked with us?"

"No."

Finally, an answer.

"No problem, just this way."

I usher the group towards a table. When we arrive the Dad stands still, not taking a seat.

"I'm not happy," he says.

"Pardon?"

"Not this table."

"Um, okay, where will you like to seat?"

Without answering me, the Dad storms off towards a corner booth on the other side of the restaurant. The same table the Finn family sat at last night. I hastily follow behind with the menus, flustered at the Dad's sudden movements.

He's a thick man, built like a short bulky tree. Bald and sweaty. He's shorter than me and he doesn't have a neck. I'm being serious, no neck. It's like his head joins into his shoulders. He doesn't smile at me at all. In fact, I think his only expression in life is a disapproving frown. That's certainly all he's giving me, anyway. He just looks like a giant egg. An egg-shaped Dad.

The family sits around the booth and I hand out the menus. I turn to leave them to peruse through when the Dad lifts up his hand and clicks his fingers at me.

Clicks. His. Fingers.

I'm so shocked by the action that I don't get angry. I just turn back around and blink at him. Confused.

I should've been angry. In fact, I should've been *irate*.

But it's so callow, so *rude* of an action that I'm in complete shock at this man.

"Beer for me," he barks, as if clicking his fingers at me was a perfectly normal and reasonable thing to do.

I scuttle off, back to the bar to follow his order like a *loser*.

I'm such a coward.

I stand behind the bar, inputting his drink order and trying not to cry.

Don't you dare cry, Bay. Not in front of this customer. Not in front of Cliff.

I can't believe that man has done that; it was like he's treating me not as a waitress but as his personal slave.

I don't know what to do.

Cliff, still ignoring me like a mopey teenager, pours a lager and sets it down on the bar for me to take. I carry it on a tray over to the table and place it in front of the egg-shaped man. He doesn't thank me. He doesn't acknowledge me at all.

I go back to behind the bar and let out a deep breath.

Don't cry. Don't cry. Don't cry.

I check on Cliff. He's pouring drinks and still pretending like I don't exist.

This is terrible.

I head out of the bar and rush into the bathroom, quickly locking the door behind me. I stare at myself in the mirror and *will* myself to not cry. I don't need makeup streaming down my face in the middle of my shift.

I think about the horrible customer out there, and the way he clicked his fingers at me.

But, most of all, I think about Cliff. About that handsome man who's ignoring me like I'm dirt. He makes me *feel* like dirt.

It's like this man won't stop until he tears my heart out.

Does he want revenge on how I threw water on him? Does he hold on to grudges that hard?

I don't know what he's thinking.

I sigh and wash my hands in the sink, staring at my reflection.

I want to quit. I want to rip off my apron right now and throw it into Cliff's stupidly handsome face.

But I won't. That'll mean he wins this little weird passive-aggressive game going on between us.

And you still need the money, Bay. You need Rockpool. You won't be hired anywhere else in this small town.

I'm right. I just need to suck this up and bear it.

* * *

THE REST of the night slowly devolves worse and worse.

I take the food order from the egg-man's table, asking around for each customer's individual choice. Even though he's on a table with his wife and four daughters, the Dad doesn't do the gentlemanly and chivalrous thing and let them go first. No. He speaks over his wife and orders ahead of her. I raise my eyebrows at this, but cover my face with my notepad, maintaining my waitress professionalism. But it's my real pet peeve as a server to see people, especially men, talk over others and order first.

It's not like your food's going to come any quicker because of it, pal. Just be nice.

I take their order and skip back to the bar so I can put their food choices through the computer system, happy to get away from that toxic table.

I head off to serve the other customers in the restaurant but always keeping a watchful eye on the troublesome table, making sure that Dad isn't up to any mischief.

I feel Cliff's own eyes on me. Even though he's still making an effort to purposely ignore me, I feel him watching me as I work around the different tables. There aren't many customers in the restaurant, it's still so quiet in here, but busy enough that I'm always moving. Grabbing cutlery, or food, or a drinks order. I'm always on the move.

Dominika rings the bell as a calling for me to collect more plates from the kitchen.

This must be the Dad's table. This must be their food.

But I can't get the food right away. I'm currently holding a tray of drinks.

The alcohol I'm carrying is for a table near the kitchen, so what I can do is take these drinks to their table and head into the kitchen to collect the plates on one long trip.

Easy.

I rush towards the kitchen, past the egg-shaped Dad's table. He is in the midst of a long rambling story, something about some big fish he caught on a boat in the ocean. He's waving his arms around as he demonstrates how big this fish was, his teenage daughters looking bored at his exaggerated story. Judging from the expressions on their faces, I bet they've heard this particular fishing tale a billion times.

As I pass the back of his chair, the Dad's energetic arm springs out in another demonstration of the size of the fish and slams into me.

Causing me to tip the tray of drinks.

Causing me to fall.

As I collapse, my waitressing instincts leap to the fore and I try my hardest to keep the glasses from smashing into the customers and instead away from them. I am successful in not letting any of the drinks hurt my customers, but I am not successful in not allowing any liquid to be splashed over the Dad as I tumble to the ground.

Both he and I are covered in beer. I slip to the floor, my ass bearing the full thrust of the impact.

Ouch.

But I'm not worried about myself, I'm concerned about the drinks.

I glance up and everything's in slow motion. All the glasses have smashed on the ground around me and not over any of the customers, so that's good, but beer has sprayed completely over the Dad and me.

I smell lager dripping from my nose.

My shirt is wet. Sticky.

Oh no.

I quickly rise back up to my feet, glancing at the damage.

No one seems hurt. The women at the table seem like they didn't even get a single drop on them.

But for me and the Dad?

Yeah, we're soaking in beer.

"I'm so sorry," I hastily mutter to the Dad, balancing myself on my feet and careful not to hurt myself on the broken glass scattered around me.

He glares up at me in shock. He's not as wet as I am, but the beer is definitely dripping down his shirt and head, leaving his bald scalp shining under the restaurant lights.

"What the *fuck*?" he whispers.

"I am so sorry," I repeat. "Let me find something to clean this up for you."

The Dad stares at me with his little beady eyes. "What the fuck are you doing?" he asks.

"I saw the whole thing," his daughter says, leaning across the table. "It was an accident. She didn't mean to spill those."

The Dad either doesn't hear her or purposefully ignores her and instead suddenly reaches out with his pudgy hand and grips me by the shirt, standing. With force, he pulls me in close to his face by my shirt. His permanent frown is turned into a menacing snarl.

What the hell?

"I want you to pay for this," he says to me quietly under his breath. "I want you to pay me for my expensive clothes you've ruined and for the way you've treated me."

I try to struggle against his grip, but he's too strong. He has me by the shirt, nearly lifting my whole body into the air. His other hand raises above me, curled in a fist.

Oh my god, he's really going to hurt me.

He's really going to hurt me.

Then suddenly, out of nowhere, a hand wraps around the Dad's arm and yanks him away from me. I'm let go and fall back on my feet. I spin around to see who's set me free.

Cliff Finn.

He's standing to my side, gripping the customer's arm, and with an expression on his face I've never seen from him before.

Pure, unbridled *anger*.

And not directed at me.

Directed at the Dad.

"Get away from her," Cliff warns the customer, his voice low. A primitive growl that's full of protection and violence.

Protection for me.

Cliff's come to my rescue.

He's stepped into harm's way for *me*.

"Who the fuck are you?" the Dad snipes at Cliff, but his attempt at a threat bounces off my boss.

"You're leaving," Cliff replies, still holding onto the man's arm. Cliff's other hand takes mine in his and guides me safely around behind him. He doesn't let go of my hand. His fingers interlock around mine.

And I feel secure. Cliff's protecting *me*. It's like nothing can harm me now.

"I said," barks the customer. "Who the *fuck* are you?"

"It doesn't matter who I am. You're leaving. Now."

"No," the Dad replies. "Not until she pays for what she did."

"She's not paying for anything."

"Oh, really?"

"Yes, *really*. Now get out of here."

"What you're gonna do about it, big man? Huh?"

Cliff stands tall, his broad shoulders squaring off against the egg-shaped bald man. "We could take this outside, but we both know that'll be pretty devastating. For you, that is."

The man looks Cliff up and down, as if seeing his muscular frame for the first time. I think I see him gulping in terror.

Oh, he's not going to try to fight Cliff.

"You think you're so tough, big guy?"

"Don't you even *dare* threaten her."

"She's just a waitress. Why should you care about her?"

"She's *my* waitress and don't you dare say anything bad about her or there'll be hell to pay."

"Look at you, defending her honor or something. You really think you're her knight in shining armor, don't you?"

"You really want to take this outside? I'm more than happy to oblige you."

"Okay, we're going," the customer sniffs. "But I'm not coming back here again."

"Good. You're not welcome."

The Dad hurries out of the restaurant like a little crab, completely leaving behind his wife and daughters to follow him on their own without him. The daughters look at us with concerned sympathy, wordlessly apologizing for their dad's behavior. I'm more sympathetic for them having to live with such a horrible man.

Once they go, Cliff lets go of my hand and walks away as if nothing happened.

He saved me, but now he's ignoring me.

He put himself in danger just to disappear on me again.

What is that man thinking?

Does he hate me, or does he like me?

What did the egg-shaped man mockingly call Cliff?

Her knight in shining armor.

13

BAY

THAT'S IT; I'm going to say *thank you* to Cliff Finn. It's taken me the rest of the shift to come to that decision, but I've made it now and I'm going to stick by it.

I hope he takes it kindly.

After that horrible customer left, the rest of the shift has gone by without a hiccup. I cleaned the broken glass, wiped down the table, and changed shirts. I always keep a spare work one in times of crises like this. I've been a waitress for so long that a little spillage of lager over me isn't the end of the world. It's not ideal, but I can learn to live with just washing myself down in the bathroom and enduring one or two more hours of the shift.

Cliff hasn't spoken to me after the *incident*. He resumed his regularly scheduled sulking and has completely refused to acknowledge me.

But that's okay. He can't hide his true side from me anymore.

Maybe Dominika was right when she said she thinks he likes me.

Someone who hates my guts wouldn't stand up for me the way he did.

Someone who likes me would've leaped to my defense.

Someone who hates me wouldn't have held my hand the way Cliff had done.

And don't get me wrong, I'm not some kind of *damsel in distress*, but the chivalrous way that Cliff stood in front of that man and defended me makes my heart jump. It's a natural instinct when you see such a handsome guy do something completely selfless for you. A guy who you think would never raise a hand to help you but who jumps in between a raised fist and you at the first sign of trouble.

And then he went back to ignoring me.

But I can live with that because I know what he's really like. He revealed himself to me, whether he wanted to or not.

And I like it.

And that's why I've made the decision, after pondering on it for the rest of my shift, to say thanks to Cliff Finn. To tell him that I appreciate what he did back there, to let him know that I honestly - *genuinely* – want to thank him for protecting me in the restaurant.

With the end of the shift and decision made, I head downstairs to the restaurant staff room, take my bag, and sneak up towards the manager's office. The last I saw of Cliff was his muscular frame heading into that room, presumably to do some late-night paperwork.

So that's where I go.

I make it outside the open door to the office when I start to hear voices. All the customers are gone. The rest of the restaurant is empty, the lights are turned off and I'm walking in darkness. But I hear voices coming from the manager's office.

Cliff and Dominika's voices.

I pause by the partially open doorway, unable to be seen from inside, and press my ear to the wall to listen.

Yeah, it's definitely them.

And Dominika's crying.

"They said it happened this morning," she's saying through tears. "He passed away this morning."

"I'm so sorry to hear that," I hear Cliff replying, his voice soft and soothing.

"I knew he was a little sick, but this is so sudden."

"It is."

"I can't believe it."

Why's she crying? Someone's passed away?

"It's always hard when a parent passes away," Cliff says.

"I mean, I wasn't even close to dad, but it's still so upsetting."

Oh, her dad.

Dominika's dad passed away.

I sigh and lean against the wall. That's really sad. I like Dominika a lot, so hearing her cry is distressing. I don't know what to do, either burst through the door like an oaf and offer my sympathies, or just leave now?

What would be the right thing to do?

But before I get the chance to think about it, Cliff starts talking again.

"Obviously, you're going to have to fly home as soon as possible."

Dominika sniffs. "I can't leave you here alone to manage the restaurant. The whole place will fall apart within days."

Cliff laughs. "That might be true, but I think I'll manage alright. I'm a big boy."

"It's okay. I'll stay. You need me."

"You can't stay here, Dominika. You have to be with your family back home."

"But this is my home."

It's sweet how Cliff's pushing her to go home over the needs of the restaurant. It's a tender side of him I don't see, the way he consoles Dominika. A side of him I didn't see until today when he saved me from that customer and is now putting Dominika's family above his business.

There is definitely more to him than meets the eye.

"You need to head home and look after your mother, Dominika. Look, I'll book you the next flight out tomorrow."

"You can barely cook, Cliff. How can you manage this restaurant without me?"

"I'll try."

"Have you checked the financial records lately? We are absolutely fucked if customers don't pick up. You can't do this on your own."

"I have checked the financial records. I was at the bank the other day trying to sort out some kind of loan."

Ah, so that's why Cliff was at the bank when I first met him.

"The bank?"

"Yeah."

"Seriously, Cliff?"

"I know what you're saying, but I won't use my family's money. Not now, not ever."

That's why he was aggressive and impatient at the bank. He was trying to fix his failing restaurant without the help of his rich family.

That explains it.

"Okay, but you need all hands on deck," Dominika protests. "You need chefs in the kitchen and waiters out front. I can't go, especially not now."

"Don't worry about the restaurant," Cliff replies forcefully. "The important thing is for you to get home and to take care of your family the same way you've taken care of me."

The restaurant is on the precipice of failing, and Dominika needs to return home.

This restaurant is the only job I can get at the moment.

I can't lose it.

This is my chance.

I need to do something.

I lean forward and knock on the open door. They both go silent as I poke my head around the corner. They both stare back at me as I open my mouth to speak.

"Sorry," I say, giving a faint smile. "I couldn't help but overhear."

"Bay?" Cliff asks, surprised. "We thought you'd gone."

I turn my attention to Dominika. Tears stream down her face. I can tell she needs a good hug, so I cross into the room and wrap my arms around her. She buries her face into my shoulder, and I whisper into her ear. "I'm so sorry for your loss."

I feel her head nodding. "Thank you," she sighs.

"You okay?"

"Yep."

"It's sad news."

"Yep."

I let her go and dig deep into my bag for a tissue, handing it over to her. Dominika dries her eyes and smiles at me. I smile back.

I love her.

I turn to Cliff. He's been standing still the whole time, not knowing what to do. I guess displays of emotion and affection like this are something he's not used to.

"I can help," I say. "I can help run Rockpool."

"What?" Cliff stares at me blankly.

"I can help keep this business afloat. I need this place as much as you guys. I need this job."

"This is good," Dominika says.

"But you're a waitress," Cliff replies, and I can feel Dominika squeezing my hand, encouraging me. She wants me to do this.

This is my chance.

"Yeah, I am a waitress, but I also know I can cook well. I can be your chef whilst Dominika's away. I can cook for you and maybe help you look into changing the menu."

"Changing the menu?"

"Yeah," I reply. "I think I can help give it a bit of a spin."

If he's going to be cocky at me, then I'm gonna be cocky back.

I can see Cliff mulling it over in his mind. I can see he doesn't like the prospect of me helping manage the place.

"I know Bay will do a good job," Dominika chimes in. She winks at me. "She's got my approval."

Cliff shakes his head at both of us. "I want nothing to do with this. I can manage this restaurant, *and cook for it*, on my own. Without you, Bay."

"I can do this, trust me."

"I don't believe you can."

"You're not even giving me a chance?"

Cliff ignores me. "Dominika," he says. "I'll book you a flight in the morning. I'll call you."

With that, he briskly leaves the office without as much as a second glance at me.

What the fuck's wrong with this man?

One moment he's putting himself into harm's way to defend me, and the next he's refusing my help. It's like he really *likes* me but also, at the same time, acts like I'm the most disgusting human on the planet.

What does he truly think of me?

"Don't worry about Cliff," Dominika says to me, squeezing my hand tight again. "He needs your help and will come around to you. Trust me."

"I hope he does. I need this job."

"Then fight for it."

"You think I should? You think it's worth it?"

"Definitely. I trust you, Bay. I know you'll do a fine job here."

I nod. "Thank you."

"You'll get to him, I know it. Plus, now you know where my secret wine stash is. You'll be able to deal with him."

I hug her again and she pulls herself in close.

"Thank you, Dominika. For everything."

"No need."

"I'm sorry about your dad."

"Me too."

"I hope going home's okay."

"Thanks, Bay," she replies. "Stick it out here, please. For me. Cliff needs you."

I scoff. "I hope you're right, because I need the job. I need the money."

14

BAY

PEARL TUGS at my hand as we pass by the toy store in the center of the shopping mall. Her little fingers pull at mine with all the force she can muster.

It isn't very effective.

"Can we go in there?" she asks, still tugging at my hand. She's trying to bring me over to the toy store.

Of course she is.

She's attracted to that place every time we're in this shopping mall, like a moth to a flame.

I crouch down so that I'm at her level. Her big eyes stare back at me. "What's the magic word, Pearl?"

Her mouth hangs open. *"Please."*

"Okay, fine."

Pearl grins at me and I allow her to pull me into the toy store, her feet running as fast as she can go on the slippery floor of the shopping mall.

As we enter the toy store, I stop her from running off.

"You're allowed to choose *one* toy, Pearl. Only one. You got that?"

"Yes."

I let her go and she predictably scrambles down the pink princess aisle, overwhelmed with all the choices in front of her. I wouldn't normally indulge her in a toy, but she's been extra good with her homework today. We had a full uninterrupted hour sitting down and working through her English textbook without any distractions, so this is her reward.

I just better not tell her dad.

But, sometimes, little cute princesses like Pearl need to be spoiled.

Especially after the past few months she's had to witness.

I wander around the toy store, checking out the different items on display, and I think back on last night, and my brazen attempt to offer help to Cliff. I hope he does accept it, even though he left in an angry rush. I hope he thinks about my offer. I am a *damn* good chef, and I know I can bring something to Rockpool. I know I can help him overhaul the menu and bring in the right changes to lure in more customers.

I just want to help.

Hopefully, he will overlook his pride and realize that.

Dominika seems to think so.

She messaged me this morning to say she's catching a flight later today back to Poland. Cliff bought it for her. I'm happy she gave in and decided that going home is what's important and not the restaurant. Looking after her family in their grief is her priority right now.

And mine is to help this restaurant.

If only Cliff will let me.

I scan my eyes over the toy displays. *Star Wars. Barbies.*

And then I see another familiar poster. A film I've seen.

The Vindicator Team.

That's the one that Cliff's ex-girlfriend's in, right? The superhero franchise I heard his cousins talking about. I stroll up to the display, observing the different toys laid out. Muscle men and robots with killer lasers. I've seen one or two of the films before, a year or so ago. They're not really my type, too much action and not enough character, but I do see the appeal if you're into superheroes.

There's another poster above the display. My eyes flicker to it.

COMING SOON. VINDICATOR WOMAN.

The image is of a tall, slim blonde woman with her hands on her hips. She's staring out into the distance with a steely look. I skim through the details on the poster, coming to a stop when I see the actress's name.

Cleo Dash.

I gasp.

That must be Cliff's girlfriend. That must be her in the poster. She's that superhero. His cousins weren't lying. She's in the new film.

I wonder what he feels about all this.

Must be hard seeing your ex's face splattered on bill-boards and posters everywhere you go. Must be hard having your ex become one of the most famous actresses on the planet in front of your eyes just months after you break up.

What does that do to someone's soul? How can their heart mend after being forced to witness something like this mere weeks after breaking up?

I know I wouldn't be able to cope.

For the first time, I feel pity for Cliff. I realize I don't really know what he's going through. No wonder he's taken out his anger on me. I held him up in that bank whilst he was trying to save the business he's invested all his time into. I humiliated him in public when he's already shamed by his ex-girlfriend rubbing her massive success in his face.

No wonder he's pissed off at me.

So why did he leap to my defense yesterday with that horrible customer?

Pearl suddenly appears, rushing at me with a toy in her hands. A princess doll.

"Another one?" I ask her as she comes to a standstill in front of me, her face beaming at her find. "Don't you have enough princesses at home?"

"Nope!"

"Really?"

"I need more."

I shrug. "Well, I guess that's fair enough. Only because you're my favorite niece in the whole world."

I take her by the hand and lead her to the tills. The cashier smiles at Pearl, clearly enamored by the girl's cuteness. I don't blame her.

"Is your mommy buying you a gift?" the cashier asks.

"I'm not..." I hasten to say, but I'm cut off by Pearl's instant rebuttal.

"My mommy's dead, but Bay is like my new mommy."

The cashier looks up in shock. She turns to me with sympathy in her eyes, speechless at what Pearl just said. My niece hugs the doll's box tight with her usual smile on her face, unaware of the chaos she's just caused. I quickly pay for the doll and mutter my thanks to the cashier. She tries to offer her apologies, but I wave my hand to stop her.

"It's okay, honestly."

I don't want her to feel bad when she doesn't know anything about Pearl's situation. And, besides, my niece doesn't seem affected at all; she doesn't seem to realize what's gone on.

Holding her hand, I take her out of the store, and I'm

shaking. It's always horrible to see Pearl talk about her mother like that. No child should ever have to do that, no child should have to process the death of a parent like it's a normal thing.

I stand in the center court of the shopping mall outside the toy store and catch my breath. Pearl is busy trying to open the box of the doll to take any notice of me.

She really is oblivious to everything that's happened.

No child as young as Pearl should talk about their mother like that.

And she called me her new mommy.

I shake my head. All I can try to do is to be there for Pearl and Davy, and be that female influence they both desperately need in their lives right now. That's all I can do.

I take in a deep breath and compose myself. I glance around the shopping mall to relax myself. Pearl, unable to open the box without my help, grabs my hand again to signal for my assistance.

And that's when I see him.

Cliff Finn.

He's standing on the other side of the shopping mall, staring at me and Pearl.

15

CLIFF

I CAN'T BELIEVE what I saw.

Bay Dover.

Bay with a child.

I didn't know she has a kid.

Does that mean she's married, or a single parent?

Well, she's successfully hidden that one from me. I haven't suspected a thing all this time. The whole time we've worked together, and I didn't know she had a child. Have I been totally blind?

Truth be told, I don't know anything about her, not much really beyond what I can glean from Dominika, and she's remained pretty sealed about the new waitress.

Dominika.

I hope she's alright. I booked her a flight back to Poland immediately upon finding out about her father's passing. I hope she made it back okay. I hope she's alright.

But she's left at the worst moment. I've tried to be brave about it in front of her, but I fully know that this restaurant will collapse without her assistance and her cooking skills. I need her. Desperately.

And then Bay offered to help.

I can't bear to have this girl around. Whenever she's in the restaurant, she's like a constant distraction for me, and I'm unable to get her out of my head. If it weren't for Dominika, I would've fired little Miss Dover by now.

But I think I like her. A lot.

And that's dangerous.

I can't have another situation like Cleo Dash happen to me again. I can't reveal my emotions to someone to just get my sincerity laughed back at me. Not again.

And that's why I can't bear to be around Bay Dover.

When that customer laid his hands on her, I instinctively sprang into action like a wild animal took control over my body. The pure protectiveness I felt for her at that moment was overwhelming. I wanted to crush that man for *daring* to touch my waitress.

For daring to touch my girl.

What had overcome me at that moment? What feelings were released that I'd kept hidden, even from myself?

I don't want to experience that again. I was too exposed. Too vulnerable. I saw in Bay's eyes that she could fully understand me at that moment.

And that terrifies me.

So, it was shocking to see her at the shopping mall with *her child.*

I didn't even think she had kids.

I didn't even think she might be in a relationship.

I have to admit, that thought sent an electric shock to my heart. Bay Dover in a relationship.

Cliff Finn, once again, laying his emotions on the chopping block just to see them get cut in half.

I knew I gotta get out of that shopping mall the minute I

saw her. I ducked out the exit and into my car, driving off towards the beach.

I needed to get Bay out of my head.

So, I went for a surf with my cousin, Cove.

* * *

"So, just a friendly surf today?" Cove asks, tapping on my car window. I've just pulled into the beach parking lot. It's midday and the sun's out. The ocean is a cool light blue and the sand's glistening white. A perfect day at the beach. "No competition then?"

"What, you're scared of my surfing skills?" I jump out of my Lamborghini, ripping off my shirt to reveal the skin-tight wetsuit underneath. Cove's already dressed for the occasion, with his professional wetsuit and carrying two surf-boards under his muscular arms. One for him and one for me.

"You're forgetting who's the pro-surfer here, cousin."

"Just because you have a few shiny trophies doesn't mean you can out-surf me, Cove."

He laughs. "We'll see about that."

Fully dressed for the waves, I take my board off my cousin and we rush down the stairs and onto the sand. We dash across the beach into the chilling water and start paddling out. In some kind of dick-measuring contest, we speed past the other surfers in the water so that we are far out at sea. Content with where we are, Cove and I sit on top of our boards and wait for a good wave.

I feel comfortable out here. There's no pressure, the stress of the restaurant is gone. It's just us two men, stripped back to only our wetsuits and wild nature. It's primal, and I love it.

But I still can't stop thinking about Bay, about how I

practically *sprinted* out of the shopping mall when I spotted her.

And I can't stop thinking about her and that kid I saw back there. Surely, it's not hers? No way.

I don't know anymore. I don't know what to think about her anymore?

I'm confused.

And I'm *never* normally confused.

"How's the restaurant going?" Cove asks me, absent-mindedly splashing the surface of the ocean with the palm of his hand.

"Let's not talk about that."

"So, really bad, then?"

"I was at the bank the other day. That's how bad it was."

"You know you can always ask your parents for help with money."

I roll my eyes. "That's not the point. I don't want the family's money anywhere near this place. I want it to succeed on its own."

"Fair enough," Cove shrugs. He turns to me, flicking his wet blonde hair away from his eyes. "And what about that cute girl that works there?"

I snort. "Who? What cute girl?"

Cove chuckles. "You know what cute girl I mean, the same girl you couldn't take your eyes off for the entire time we were there the other night. That girl."

I shake my head in denial, but I know my cheeks are inflaming. I'm flushing. *Jesus.* Is this what the thought of Bay does to me now? "She's on a whole other level."

"What do you mean?" Cove asks.

Should I tell him about my feelings? I do trust him. He is my cousin, after all.

"I just don't know what to think about her. One

moment she has me angry, then the next she has my heart pounding. I don't know what to think about her."

"Was it the same with Cleo?"

I sigh. "Cleo and I were a good match."

"Yeah," Cove replies, frowning. "But does that mean you actually *fancied* each other, or were you just a good couple on paper?"

"Well, Cleo didn't make me feel like what Bay's making me feel now, if that's what you mean."

Cove laughs. "I think you fancy the poor waitress then, Cliff. I think that is what's happening."

"Jesus Christ."

"No, it's an improvement for you. I remember the days when all you were doing was fucking your way around Europe."

"Yeah, and you weren't much different back here. What's the nightclub called?"

Cove rolls his eyes. "Tide."

"Yeah, you were like the playboy *king* of that place."

"You're right there, and then I met Ripley."

"It was different times. I've grown up now, no more Europe and no more Tide. I've grown up."

"So have we all," Cove says. "Maybe this waitress might be your Ripley. Maybe she'll get you out of this funk you're in."

I growl. "Shut up, loser."

But maybe he's right.

Maybe I need Bay.

No, you don't.

Why does she make me so confused? I'm usually so level-headed, so why does she make my stomach fall into a spin every time I think about her? I can't see straight.

"Here one comes," Cove whispers excitedly as he gazes

out towards the horizon. He's right. A giant wave's coming. "I'll race you to the shore."

"I thought you said this was a friendly surf? No competition?"

"Oh, I've changed my mind."

I smile. "Well, this'll be easy, then."

"Will it now?"

"Right. Let's race."

16

CLIFF

I STAND in the middle of the restaurant kitchen with the menu in my hands, sighing. I squint to look at the writing on the paper.

There's too much to take in. Too many items and I don't even know what half of them contain.

This is hopeless.

Somehow, with no cooking credentials or training at all, I'm meant to overhaul this menu into something that will attract a new load of customers.

Great.

Something tells me that isn't going to happen.

Fuck.

Frustrated, I drop the menu onto the kitchen counter and rub my forehead. I bite my tongue and glance over at the kitchen utensils laid out before me. I don't even know what half of them can even do, let alone dare to use them to whip up a whole new batch of best-selling dishes.

I have absolutely zero training in cooking.

Why did I think I'll ever be able to manage this?

Manage a miracle?

Damn, Dominika. You left me at the most inopportune moment.

I hear the *whoosh* of the kitchen doors swing open behind me, and I turn to look who it is that's dared intruded on me.

Bay has entered the kitchen. She's still wearing the same clothes as I saw her in at the shopping mall earlier. She must've come from there to here. I check the clock. It is time for her to start her shift.

Well, there's no point in her starting now. There are no customers. And no menus.

"Hi," she smiles at me. I know she's been extra cheerful with me the past couple of days. I hate it. I hate how she's trying to make me act all *nice* towards her.

But I can't resist her smile; she makes me feel butterflies in my stomach that I can't control. I'm all fluttery when I see her smile. It's a very pretty smile, full of sunshine, and I hate how she can make me feel like this.

"Hello, Bay," I begrudgingly reply. She seems to light up that I've acknowledged her.

"How's the menu coming along?"

"I don't need your help," I reply.

"I'm just asking."

I roll my eyes and drop my shoulders. She's *persistent*, I'll give her that. "Not good," I say. And that's the understatement of the year.

"Can I have a look at it?"

Bay doesn't wait for my answer before she comes strutting over to me. She leans over my shoulder to read the menu. She's so close I can smell her sweet perfume. She even *smells* like sunshine. Can this girl get any sweeter?

She's so close it's like there's a spark of electricity between us, a tension I can't avoid.

Who is this girl to inspire such dormant feelings within me?

I've never felt this nervous or charged with energy with any other girl, and I'm the guy who's slept with half of Europe. Supermodels and actresses and nobility - I've fucked them all - but none have affected me like this waitress.

What is it with Bay Dover?

I turn to Bay and try to hold in my desire to touch her, to kiss her soft lips. "I need you outside waitressing, not here in the kitchen," I say.

"There's no one out there," she replies, lifting her chin. "I *can* cook, and I can help you if only you'd allow me to."

Fine.

"Alright then," I say, stepping away from her. "Show me your cooking if you're so keen. Show me your skills."

"Show you?"

"Yeah," I reply. "Show me that you can cook. My favorite food is a nice medium-rare steak. How about you rustle one up for me?"

She eyes me suspiciously. "You're serious?" she asks.

"Oh, yes I am."

"Right here? Right now?"

"Make me a good steak and then we'll see how good you are."

"Alright." Bay flicks her hair back and turns to the sink, washing her hands with soapy water. She's trying to appear confident with the way she glides over to the kitchen counter and checks around for the right cooking equipment, but I know she's nervous. Good. I want her to be. She talks the good talk. Let's see if she can pull this off.

It'll be good to embarrass her if she's not even that good after all.

"Medium rare?" she asks.

"Yep."

"Got it."

I watch Bay as she circles around the kitchen, spinning from counter to counter and the fridge to grill as she slowly prepares herself. I cross my arms, hoping to be a watchful nuisance.

She turns to me. "How about you take a step back, Cliff?"

I raise my hands up. "Sure."

I give her the space to work around me. I watch her as she cooks a nice cut of steak we've stored in the fridge. I watch her cute brown hair sway as she speeds around the kitchen. I watch the softness of her lips as she works and her lovely intense green eyes as she closely observes what she's doing.

The girl's very pretty, I'll give her that.

She's not like a supermodel, but she's more *real*. Not someone I would normally fancy, but *here we are*. I like how she handles the food, the way she plays with it. I don't want to admit it, but she knows what she's doing. She's got this under control.

I like her.

Dammit. It was never supposed to come to this. I told myself never again after what happened with Cleo. *No more girls*, I told myself after that Paris hotel room. *Don't expose your heart like that.*

But Bay Dover has swanned into my life and is tearing open my heart like she's currently doing with the steak in front of her.

What have I got myself into?

"*Ta da,*" she exclaims, and I blink, snapping out of my daydream.

She's done.

"You're finished?" I ask.

"Yep."

"No way."

"I'm all done."

She spins around and offers me a plate. She's cooked a steak and smothered it in garlic sauce. I take a peek at it, then at her. Bay is biting her lip, waiting for my reaction.

She looks kinda cute like that.

I place the steaming plate on the kitchen counter, pick up my steak knife, and cut it open.

It's cooked perfectly to medium-rare, just pink enough. The way I like it.

Damn, she's good.

I take a bite.

The flavor explodes in my mouth and I find myself drooling for the rest of it.

Shit, she's really good.

No way.

Bay can really cook.

"What do you think?" she asks, nervous.

Great, now I have to admit that she's actually a natural at this.

"Yeah. Good." I grunt back at her, and Bay's eyes light up. She knows what I think, and now she's over the moon with joy. And smugness.

"See, what did I tell you?"

"Yeah, I'll give you this. You can cook, Bay Dover."

She smiles at me and sways back and forth on her heels. "See?"

I take another bite of the steak. I can't resist it, the food is just that good.

"I see it, just don't go rubbing it in my face."

"I wouldn't dream of it," she replies. "So, will you hire

me as a chef, then?"

"What?"

"Hire me as a chef, now that you can taste how good I am."

"I'm not looking for a chef."

"I know there's been a recent vacancy in the position, and I also know I don't have many contenders for the job."

"You're cheeky," I reply.

But she's right.

She is good.

And I need a chef. I *really* can't do this on my own.

Bay looks up at me expectedly. "So?"

"Sure," I mutter.

"And that means a pay rise?"

Oh.

"Now you're really getting cheeky."

"I can't spend all my time here, making up a new menu, on just my waitressing rates."

"So you want a pay rise?"

"Yep."

I sigh. "Alright."

"Perfect." She raises her eyebrows.

"You drive a hard bargain, Miss Dover."

"That I do. But you need me."

She's won.

I get it.

She's proved herself. Good for her.

I'm man enough to admit it when I've lost. Bay *can* cook.

"So," she says. "What do I do? When do I start?"

"Come round to my apartment tomorrow at noon," I reply. "We can work through a new menu."

Bay nods, and I know that I'm going to have to eat the rest of the steak before I leave. It's just that good.

17

BAY

I'M HELPING Pearl play with her dolls in the living room when my brother walks in with a panicked look on his face. Davy's on the sofa, playing his Nintendo Switch but he puts it down, worried, when his stressed-out dad flies in.

I glance up from the doll set Pearl and I are playing with when Fisher enters. "What's wrong, Fisher?" I ask.

"Work's just called," he replies, looking at Pearl sitting on the living room floor with her dolls. "They need me to come in today, right now. There's been a gas leak and I'm the only one who can fix it."

Work?

Fisher had today off. This was meant to be his day with the kids.

"You've been called in?"

"Yeah," Fisher replies. "Can you do me a massive favor and take care of Pearl and Davy for me today?"

"It's meant to be your day off. Isn't there anyone else that can sort this out?"

"I know, and I can't," my brother says, his face down-trodden. "But work sounded pretty urgent. I need to go in. I'm really the only one who can fix this."

"Daddy?" Pearl asks, her big round eyes pleading with him. She doesn't fully understand what's happening yet, but she knows her dad's got bad news. "Where are you going?"

Fisher leans down to her level. "I need to visit work, honey. They really need me right now."

"You said you were going to play dolls with us."

He takes her tiny hand in his and strokes it. "I know, sweetie, but daddy has to go into work."

"Okay," Pearl lowers her face, unable to conceal the sadness in her voice.

She really loves her daddy.

She needs to spend time with him.

"I'm sorry, Bay," my brother says, turning to me. "Are you able to do me this massive favor?"

"Okay," I reply. I know why he has to go in, but it's disappointing he has to leave his kids behind. Another day of them without their dad on top of all the other days of the week he works.

It's not good for them.

"You're a superstar," Fisher replies to me, hastily ushering himself out the front door. I don't expect him to leave so quickly. By the time I stand up, I can already hear his car zooming off down the street.

And then I remember.

What I have to do today. Why I can't take care of the kids.

Cliff's house.

Oh, shit.

I have to go to Cliff's place and help him with the menu. That's supposed to be today.

Oh, crap.

I agreed to do it because I thought I'll be free without the kids today. But that's not happening anymore.

But I need this job. Cliff's giving me a chance here that I can't afford to miss.

I'm just gonna have to go to his.

And I have no choice but to bring my niece and nephew.

"Right, guys," I say, spinning around to Davy and Pearl. "Who's up for a little adventure?"

* * *

I FOLLOW the instructions on my phone to get to Cliff's place. He lives by the ocean, in the posh area of town. The expensive street with all the tall white houses that face onto the water.

How very typical of him to live here.

I park the car on the street outside his address and turn around to the kids.

"Okay, guys. The person we're about to see is my big boss."

"The scary one?" Pearl asks, interrupting me.

I smile. "Yes, the super scary one. But don't worry, I'm here to look after you from him. I just need you both to be on your best behavior."

In the back seat, Davy harrumphs. He's not happy with me saying *best behavior*. He doesn't like those two words because it usually means the opposite of what he wants to do. Pearl just blinks at me from the front passenger seat. She doesn't really know how to control her behavior, so no matter what I say, she'll just ignore me, anyway.

Well, this is going to be very interesting.

"Okay, Davy?" I ask him, raising my eyebrows. "Best behavior, alright? No shooting games or running around."

He eyes me angrily.

"Why do we have to be here?" he asks.

"Because your dad had to go to work, and I have to meet my big boss, that's why," I reply. "So, let's just get in there, get this over with, and then we can go home and play video games."

With difficulty, I escort the two out of the car. Pearl's keen to hold my hand whilst Davy just kicks at the grass, bored and irritated. We head up the stone path to the white house's front door and I take in a deep breath.

Here goes.

I ring the doorbell and take a step back, nervous. Pearl squeezes my hand.

It takes a long while before the door opens.

And there he is.

In a suit, the sleeves rolled up exposing his muscular forearms, he stands at the doorway and stares in wonderment at Pearl and Davy by my legs.

"Hello," he whispers, aghast at the sight of the kids.

Great.

"Hi, Cliff. This is Pearl and Davy. Pearl and Davy, this is Cliff Finn, my boss."

Pearl hides behind my leg, sucking her thumb, and Davy looks away, uninterested.

"Well, say hello, guys," I say.

"Hello, mister," Pearl sweetly singsongs, scared of the big, tall man. Davy just grunts something inaudible.

And Cliff just glares at them.

"Well," I say to the man. "Are you going to say hello back?"

Cliff's eyes sparkle with bewilderment, and maybe a touch of anger. I can't tell. "Hi." Without another word, he turns and disappears into the house, leaving us to follow behind. I bite my lip, worried.

Cliff doesn't seem very happy to see them.

He leads us into the main living area of the beachside property. The place is completely empty except for a few gym weights and a single basic chair in the middle of the living room. No TV. No artwork. Just white walls, some weights, and a single chair. A few surfboards lean propped up against a wall.

Wow. Cliff Finn's taking the term "bachelor pad" to the extreme here.

A few months of living here and this is what he's chosen to decorate his expensive house with?

Clearly, there's been no woman's touch in here.

What's happened in his past to make him live like this?

I bring the kids into the center of the room, next to the chair. On one side of the room is the kitchen, a large modern and minimalistic space, and dominating the other side is the wall-length window and doors leading out into a long sloping garden into the beach.

It's an amazing location. Shame about the interior décor.

All you can see outside is the white sand and the blue ocean flowing out into the horizon. A blue sea and blue skies.

Cliff stands awkwardly by the massive window, his back to us.

"I'm sorry I've brought the kids," I say.

He turns to me. "They can play in the backyard."

Davey's face lights up and, as if given a cue, sprints out the door and onto the lawn, playing. Pearl, still afraid of Cliff and sucking her thumb, gingerly follows her brother outside.

I shrug at Cliff and wait anxiously for what he's going to say next. I feel like I've surprised him, caught him off guard, and that he doesn't like that I've brought the kids here.

Maybe he doesn't even like children. Maybe he hates them being in his house.

"I'm sorry about them," I repeat. "Their dad had to go into work."

"Are they yours?" he asks. "You never told me you had kids."

"What?"

"The kids, are they yours?"

Oh.

So that's why he's annoyed.

He thinks they're mine.

"No," I reply.

"You're married?"

His tone is sharp and angry.

Wait, he's annoyed because he thinks I'm married and have a family?

Does that mean he likes me? He's doesn't hate the kids; he's just upset that it might mean I'm married?

Is this what's been bothering him today? Does this explain all the angry glances at me and the kids?

Oh.

"I'm not married, Cliff," I reply, flashing my ringless hand. His eyes glaze over me, thinking. "Pearl and Davy are my brother's kids."

Cliff's face slumps. Recognition flitters across it.

He understands now.

I'm not married. He understands the kids aren't mine. He understands he made an unfair and mistaken assessment of me.

I bet he feels like a right idiot, almost berating me like that. Thinking I have kids I haven't told him about.

That explains that shocked and irate expression he shot

at me from across the shopping mall yesterday. He thought Pearl was mine, and that I was hiding the fact of her existence from him for some reason.

Well, he was wrong.

"I'm sorry," he says, and I know he's sincere. "I thought they were yours. I thought you were married."

"Well, I'm not."

I don't really want to rub in his mistake, especially seeing how embarrassed he looks. But he did act so annoyed when I arrived with them in tow, it's hard not to make him feel sorry for how he's treated us.

"I'm a right idiot," Cliff says.

"Yes, you are."

"Please forgive me."

"Don't act like you're in a Jane Austen novel," I reply. "Let's just move past it."

"Sure."

Davy runs back into the living room from the backyard, full of energy. Brave, he sprints over to Cliff and tugs at his pants. A little whirlwind of built-up energy.

"Are you Bay's boyfriend?" he asks Cliff, bursting with that blunt confidence of a kid.

Cliff opens his mouth, flustered.

He's clearly not dealt with many kids before. He's not spent much time around them.

I like it. I like how embarrassed he's become in the last few minutes. First the realization that Pearl and Davy are not my kids, that I'm not secretly married, and now his pitiful attempts to answer my nephew's awkward question.

"I'm... uh, her *boss*."

"But you can still be boyfriend and girlfriend."

"She's just my... *friend*."

"Ew, you can't just be friends with a girl."

"Yes, you can."

"Is she your friend, or is she your *girlfriend?*"

I stand there in the middle of Cliff's living room, watching him flounder his way through my nephew's incessant interrogation. I cross my arms and smile, very much enjoying this spectacle.

It's good to see Cliff Finn humbled, especially by a child.

The man thinks he's so high and mighty. He's an international playboy with a billionaire family, yet he's being overcome by a young boy's questioning.

I like seeing him like this.

He's cute.

"Okay, Davy," I say, rescuing Cliff. "Time to go outside. Play with your sister. Mr. Finn and I have work to do."

Davy runs to Pearl and Cliff lets out a sigh of obvious relief.

"You helped me out there."

I laugh. "Okay, *friend.*"

Cliff shakes his head and gestures to the kitchen.

"Let's get started, shall we?"

We first make a soup together, something I learned about in another restaurant I worked at. It was a best-seller there, and I think it'll go well with Rockpool. As I make it, Cliff brings out the restaurant's menu and we slowly go through it. Checking each item. I offer my own thoughts on each one, something Cliff is open to.

I didn't expect him to be so amicable today.

He's growing on me. I can see he's becoming more accepting of me. He's really starting to respect me.

And I think he likes me.

I must've changed his mind over that fine steak I cooked him yesterday.

He has to admit I'm a good chef, that I can go the distance. He can't deny my skills any longer.

I glance up at his eyes as we scan through the menu. He looks back at me.

"I think we've onto a good start here," I say.

"I think so too," he replies.

Our hands are resting on the menu, touching.

Our bodies are close. Mere inches apart.

"So, you admit I'm actually alright?"

"Yeah," Cliff replies with a smirk. "You're *okay*."

"Shut up." I playfully punch him on the shoulder.

"You are more than okay, Bay. You're pretty good at this."

"Thanks for giving me the chance."

"Thanks for not being married.

"Again, shut up."

I forget about the soup as thoughts of Cliff consume me. His muscles. His smile. His jawline. The intensity with which his brown eyes stare back at me.

He really does look like Superman.

His biceps are the size of my body. His lips are full and welcoming.

And he's staring right back at me. I'm lost in his penetrating gaze.

"Pretty good?" I ask, my breathing shallow.

"I'd say even more than that."

I forget about everything. The soup. The menu. My niece and nephew playing outside. I'm just focused on Cliff Finn and the electricity between our touching hands.

He leans in closer, and I don't stop him.

His lips partly open, full and wet, and I let his face lean towards mine.

One thought screams repeatedly through my head.

He wants to kiss me, he wants to kiss me, he wants to kiss me.

And then he says it.

"Would it be strange if I said I want to kiss you, Bay?"

"Honestly, it wouldn't be the strangest thing you've said to me."

I suddenly know that everything in the last few days has been leading up to this. Cliff's acted so strangely around me simply because he fancies me.

And I fancy him.

"Well, then. Bay, I want to kiss you."

"I want you to kiss me, Cliff."

And, with his body enveloping mine, I let him.

And Cliff and I kiss.

18

CLIFF

I WAVE at the car from the doorway and I see Bay's little niece - Pearl; I think her name is – excitedly wave back at me from the front seat, her pigtails flying around with the biggest smile on her tiny face.

I'm not the biggest fan of kids, but even I have to admit she's very sweet.

I wait for the car to turn the corner before I shut my door and let out a sigh of relief.

They've gone.

Wow. What a morning this has been.

I didn't expect that Bay would arrive at my doorstep with two kids in tow. Two kids that I thought were hers. I didn't expect them to go running around my place. I didn't expect to get so embarrassed finding out I was wrong, that Bay wasn't married with a secret family.

But, most of all, I didn't expect that kiss.

The kiss in my kitchen.

The kiss that just happened. The kiss that felt so right.

I run my hands through my hair.

What have you gotten yourself into, Cliff?

I've fucked half of Europe, and yet this waitress-slash-chef has made me more nervous and giddier than any super-model or actress or member of nobility ever has.

What's happening with your heart, Cliff? Have you gone soft?

I head back into my living room, back into my kitchen, and I start to clean up. We made a mess, Bay and I, with the amazing soup she made. We couldn't stop touching each other, feeling each other, even when we were tasting her food. She's really cast a spell over me.

And we'd shared a *kiss*. A long, passionate kiss.

And that was it. We kissed, ate the soup, and then she left. It all seemed to happen so fast. Almost like it was awkward. I found myself saying goodbye to the kids and standing around, not knowing what to do with myself as they readied to leave.

Maybe she wanted to go.

Maybe my kiss scared her.

Maybe I fucked up.

It wouldn't be the first time. This is always what happens when I make the move, just like back in that Paris hotel room with my proposal to Cleo. Everything always goes wrong for me when I try to be genuine. When I put my heart on the line is when everything gets fucked.

And maybe it's happened again today.

Maybe that was the last time I'll see Bay Dover. Maybe I've screwed up by kissing her and she never wants to see me again.

I bet she hates me, and I know she has every reason to do so. I assumed the kids were hers. I basically accused her of being secretly married. I've treated her terribly ever since she first stepped foot inside my restaurant.

What have I done?

I wash the bowls and plates in the soapy water.

Do I actually like her?

Is that why I'm freaking out over her, over what she thinks of me?

No way, but I think I do.

I fancy Bay Dover.

She's not like other girls. She's not like Cleo Dash. Bay is good-hearted. Genuine. Smart. Sassy. Someone I want in my life.

In a few days, I've gone from hating her guts to now feeling like a schoolboy with a crush whenever she enters a room.

Who have I become?

The man who's broken a hundred hearts, now reduced to a giddy little boy when even just thinking of Bay Dover.

She has me completely.

Fuck.

I wipe down the bowels with a towel. Finished in the kitchen, I head over to my chair and slump down in it, looking out over the ocean.

One thing's for sure. Bay is an amazing cook.

I continue to just stare out over the amazing view, thinking of Bay. Thinking of her soft lips. The way she pushed into me during that kiss, like she wanted me to consume her. The way she lifted her chin up to reach my tall height.

She didn't seem to *hate* the kiss, quite the opposite. So why then did she practically run away straight afterward? Why did she disappear in a whirlwind? What did I do wrong?

And why can't I stop thinking about her?

I sit here, in my chair by the window for the next hour,

and think about this strange girl who's just entered my life but who's taken complete control over it.

And then, after a whole hour, the doorbell rings, startling me from my thoughts. I get up and head to the door.

Who can this be?

I open it.

And, speak of the devil, there she is.

Bay. Standing there on my doorstep. With no kids.

And she's holding some big bags. Shopping bags. Full of things I can't see.

"Hi," she says, smiling.

"Hello."

I can tell what she's thinking. It frightens me. Makes me nervous.

What's she doing here?

I don't understand what she's done, or why she's returned. Did she like the kiss or not? Could she not get it out of her head, like I've been unable to?

Could she not stop thinking about me, like I haven't been able to do about her?

It's only been an hour or so since she's left, and now she's returned, and I don't know what this means.

"What's all this?" I ask, nodding at the bags, but I might as well be asking what she's doing back here.

Bay continues smiling as if she knows something I don't. As if she's got a hidden ace up her sleeve. "I've dropped off the kids back home. My brother's back and he can take care of them, and then I drove by the hardware store."

"The hardware store?"

That explains where the shopping bags have come from. But why?

"Well," Bay says, peeking over my shoulder and into my house. "I was thinking you need some serious redecoration of this bachelor pad; it's just too bare. It's terrible. So, I've brought some paints and some brushes, and I was thinking we might as well start with the walls, and then we can move on to buying some furniture. How does that sound?"

I'm stunned into silence, but Bay doesn't seem to care. She doesn't wait for my response before she brushes past me into the hallway, leaving me to carry the shopping bags in.

She's back.

In my house.

After the kiss.

Alone.

And it turns out she's not just a chef, but also, apparently, an interior designer.

What's going on?

19

BAY

I'M GOING to make his house less barren. Less empty. Less like some unlived-in bachelor pad. The place looks like his soul, and I'm going to change it.

Cliff eyes me suspiciously as I size up the living room and its single chair.

When we left just an hour ago, I couldn't get Cliff out of my head. I kept on imagining him in this empty house all alone, and it pained me. I knew I needed to do something about it.

So, it was good that Fisher was home when we got back. I dumped the kids on him and immediately shot off to the hardware store, picking up some paints I think will go well in this place. I also bought myself a pair of overalls, ready to paint.

I needed to come back here and resolve this house.

Without kids.

And to also resolve that kiss we shared. The kiss that made me so... *confused*.

Cliff drops the hardware store bags in the middle of the room and waits for me to say something. I don't blame him for being confused at the sight of me. I've burst back into his house in a blur of passion ready to redecorate.

And, I think, he's still obsessing over the kiss. I know certainly I am.

I'm back to paint the house, and also to understand what the hell's just happened in Cliff's kitchen.

I didn't expect us to do that. If you told me, we would be kissing just a few days ago, I would've laughed in your face. I didn't expect him to lean over and kiss me, and I also definitely did not expect to find myself falling ravenously into it.

In that moment, when our lips touched, I realized how much I wanted it.

That was the most shocking thing of all. I wanted it. I wanted Cliff to kiss me.

But I was still so confused immediately afterward. I made the soup quickly and got the kids out of there in a panic. I didn't want to spend a moment thinking about it. I didn't know what I'd do if I did. I didn't know how I would react, so I swept the kids up and bundled them into the car, wanting to get away from the place.

But, once gone, all I wanted to do was get back to his house.

Get back to Cliff.

Oh, god. What's going on in your mind, Bay?

Have I gone mad?

Well, at least I've come back like a crappy Sherlock Holmes. Now I'll discover if my feelings were right, if it was right to kiss Cliff. If I was right in kissing back.

"You want to paint my house?" he asks me as I survey his living room.

"Sure."

"Paint?"

"Yeah, that's why I brought these," I reply, gesturing at the paint pots. "Your place is looking far too bare for my liking. You need to liven it up a little. You need a woman's touch."

"A woman's touch?"

"I was thinking about this wall here," I say to him, pointing at the side wall of the living room.

"This wall?"

"We'll try this one first as a tester, and then move on," I reply. "What do you think?"

Cliff glances at me, then at the paints, then back at me. "Sure," he says, shrugging.

Maybe he's also confused about the kiss. Maybe, like me, he also wants to find out if it wasn't just a random thing but something more.

Getting ready to paint, at the same time, we both lean over to pick out the paint pots. We laugh awkwardly at how we nearly bump heads. The air is electric between us. Tension. A slight awkwardness. I find myself bristling at it, feeling a pit of butterflies in my stomach. Nervous energy shoots up my body as I realize how close we are again, energy I like. We were this close earlier when Cliff kissed me. He must surely know that.

There's so much pent-up energy in this room, and I don't know what to do about it.

I pull up a couple of paint pots from the bags.

"What color do you reckon?" I ask.

"This one."

It's blue.

"Good choice."

I place it by the wall and reach back down into the bag for the brushes.

"Hang on," Cliff says. "I'll get dressed into something... less expensive."

He dashes off into the bedroom, leaving me alone in his living room. I let out a long sigh, a lungful of air I've been holding in since I entered. My skin tingles, on edge. My body is reacting so strongly to Cliff's presence. I'm trying to act normal, but my entire mind is just focused on his lips. The same lips that were over mine just an hour ago.

I would love to taste him again.

What am I doing? This is Cliff Finn, the guy who's played me around. The guy who insulted me then ignored me at work, then doubted my cooking abilities.

But this is also the same Cliff who rescued me from that awful customer, who's given me a chance, who admitted he was wrong about both my cooking skills and the fact he thought I was married. The same Cliff who was so *tender* towards me in the kitchen this morning, who softly held my chin with his hand as he kissed me.

There are two Cliffs.

And I don't know who the real one is.

He returns with an old hoodie on and tracksuit pants.

"Right," he says proudly. "I'm ready to paint."

We both work together, placing an old rag on the floor by the wall, opening the paint, getting the brushes ready. I keep averting my eyes away from Cliff's, afraid mine will reveal what I'm really thinking about him. About his body. About his lips.

We start painting the wall together, working as a team.

"You think the restaurant will be okay?" I ask as we work.

"Well, if we spruce up the menu, we can only hope," Cliff replies. "I was thinking of having a party once we've sorted it all out."

"Yeah?"

"A re-launch party, if you know what I mean. Invite some reviewers, some local businesses, that kind of thing."

I turn to him. "Sounds good."

There's a long pause while we both work. I don't know what to say. Days of my snarky replies back to Cliff, and now that we've kissed, I don't know how to even *speak* to him?

What's happened to me?

What's happened to the usual spikey Bay?

"Thank you," Cliff says, his back to me, the first one to break the tension.

"Thanks for what?"

"For helping," he replies. "For doing this, and the menu, and the cooking."

"You would be pretty helpless in that kitchen without me."

He laughs. "I'm sure I would be."

"And thank *you*," I say. Cliff tilts his head back at me, curious. "For saving me from that man the other day."

"No problem," he replies. "I didn't like how he was zooming in on my territory. Only I can abuse Rockpool's waitresses."

This time, it was my turn to laugh.

He's not too bad.

There's more to Cliff than I first thought there was, back at the bank the first day we met. There's more to him. Something hidden under his cocky, aggressive attitude. Something approaching kindness.

And he's also pretty damn funny.

I know something's hurt him in the past, something to do with his ex-girlfriend. Maybe that's why he was so defensive the first few times we met, and now, with the kiss we shared, I'm getting a better picture of what might've been going through his head.

"Um," I start to say as we paint, but Cliff interrupts me.

"I know what you're going to say."

"What?"

"You want to talk about that kiss?"

He's being blunt.

"Yes." I try to appear unfazed by the turn in our conversation, but my wavering voice betrays me.

We're actually talking about it.

This is what I came back here to do.

"Look, that was a mistake."

I shrug. "I don't think it was."

"You don't think so?" he asks.

"No."

Cliff exhales. There's a little bit of blue paint on his nose, and he's completely unaware of it. Makes him look cute. "Me neither. I don't know why I said I thought it was."

"We don't have to talk about this," I reply. "We can just put it behind us if you'd like."

Cliff takes in a deep breath. "I just want to say that there's been a reason why I was treating you like a dick, and it's only taken me till today - until that kiss - to fully realize why I was acting in such a stupid way."

"What reason?"

Cliff's dark brown eyes find mine. I melt under his intense glare. "I *like* you, Bay. That's the reason. I was intimidated by you, and by what I *felt* towards you. Because of that, I acted like a total dick."

I move towards him. He seems so exposed, so vulnerable. So serious and sincere. It's so addictive to see. This big, tall man reduced to a nervous wreck because he's talking to me and about how much he likes me.

I'm making him feel this.

The cocky and so-sure-of-himself Cliff Finn is exposing his heart to me.

And I can't resist.

I take another step towards him so that we are inches apart. His broad chest obscures my view. I bite my lip anxiously. He waits for my answer, uncertainty crossing his face.

"I like you too," I whisper.

And Cliff can't hear what I've said.

"Pardon?"

I look up at him. Up at his dark brown eyes waiting anxiously for my answer.

"I like you too," I repeat.

And then he kisses me. For the second time today.

Our lips meet in an explosion of excitement within me, and I am in a state of heightened arousal.

He likes me.

He was just so intimidated by me, and his feelings for me, that he acted like a dick.

Now I understand.

I feel his thick arms around me. I drop my paintbrush and embrace him back. We're covered in paint, but neither of us cares.

"I can't believe this is happening," I say.

"Well, believe it," Cliff replies.

"You're a good kisser."

Cliff winks and brings me back into a kiss. "That's because I have a good partner."

He pulls me up and I jump around him, wrapping my legs around his waist. Cliff doesn't react to my full body weight resting on him. He can take it. His hands stroke my hair and keep me securely in place as we continue kissing. I feel his tongue inside my mouth, and I let him enter me.

I'm going to make the first move here.

I rip away at his hoodie, bringing it over his head so that

he is just bare-chested. His body's warm. I feel his muscles. His abs. The straight blunt lines leading down to his pants.

I'm so turned on.

Responding to my need for him, Cliff brings me down to the ground so that I'm lying on my back. Balanced on the old rag we've put on the floor to protect it from the paint, I reach out for his tracksuit pants, pulling them down.

Cliff smiles when his cock falls out. Erect and big.

My eyes widen at his member.

That's going into me?

"You want this?" Cliff asks with a wink.

I sigh. "*Yes,*" is all I manage to say.

Cliff leans over and helps me out of my paint-stained overalls until I'm just in my bra and panties.

"I want you," Cliff whispers as we both stare at each other's bodies. He looks like a marble Greek statue. All lines and muscles. His jawline is simply *criminal*.

I can't hold back any longer. "I want you so much, Cliff."

There, I've said it.

I've said what has been bubbling underneath. It's the truth. I want him.

"I want all of you, Cliff."

"You can have me," he replies.

And then he rips off my panties and I feel his finger softly touch my skin, tracing its way up to my sex.

His finger finally enters me, and I gasp in pleasure. I feel him penetrate deep inside me, making me squirm as he smiles.

I close my eyes as he plays with my clit, lost in my image of Cliff. Lost in the thoughts of how he rescued me from that customer the other day. That strength. His threat of violence towards the man. His protectiveness. And now he's being so soft and tender with me.

His finger keeps digging deeper within me as I feel his lips graze mine. I open my eyes to see Cliff above me.

"I'll be back in a moment," he whispers.

And then he lets go of me and I moan in displeasure.

I want him to keep going.

"Come back," I groan as Cliff smiles and disappears into his bedroom.

But, like he said, a moment later he reappears, condom in hand.

Oh.

"I'm going to go inside you, Bay," he says as he strolls back on over. I drink in his naked body. His athletic and muscular body.

He's coming straight for me.

He kneels down, fitting the condom over her large cock.

And then he enters me.

20

BAY

I ROLL up against Cliff's naked body as we lie here and make myself at home. His sweat is hot and strangely welcome. I love feeling his solid muscles and the heat emanating from his body. It just makes me want to smuggle up here against him and never, ever leave.

And I'm planning not to.

Not for a long time, at least.

We're lying in his bed post the greatest sex I've ever had in my life. Ever. We moved in here when we finished, deciding the bed was a much more comfortable option than the old paint rag we'd just dirtily fucked on. I'm all soft and drowsy from the incredible sex, like his body's made me drunk. I'm *exhausted*, but so deeply satisfied. The man can *fuck*, to put it bluntly.

The man knows how to press my buttons.

The way he thrust inside me, he *dominated* me. Dominated my world. He moved so elegantly as he fucked me. I found myself watching his body move with each thrust of his pelvis, watching him and his thick legs sway as he grunted and moaned. I liked how he desired me, the force he unleashed, and how tired he was. And still, he fucked like a wild animal.

And I was no different. I'm sure I've made scratch marks down his back with my pleasure. Even if I have, Cliff's strong enough not to acknowledge it. I couldn't help myself. He's so strong and all-encompassing. He dominated me, and I let him.

I would never have believed you if you told me a few days ago in that bank that I'd be screwing the brains out of that rude Superman and actually *enjoying* it.

But I have.

And it feels *great*.

Out of this world.

What a beautiful and passionate man. His touch had been so tender and soft, yet so direct and aimed to give me the most amount of pleasure. He knew what he was doing, that's for sure. He knew how to make me come.

And come I did.

Lying in his bed, I snuggle in closer, my head resting against his enormous bicep. He stirs, but I'm unable to see his face from where I'm lying close to his firm chest.

"You really need to change things in here," I whisper, blinking around his sparse bedroom.

"What do you mean?" he asks, his voice low and quiet. It's good to know he's also exhausted due to our lovemaking. I'm glad I've made this six-foot-something hunk of a man tired from just my body.

"Well, your walls could use some paint for a start. Liven up the room."

"Not more paint. Please, no more."

"You need to spruce up this room. And then we could

actually fit in some furniture. There's space for a wardrobe here, not just a rack with your suits hanging up."

Even though he's a rich man, Cliff's gone out and clearly just bought a cheap rack to hang his clothes. It's not a wardrobe, just a flimsy plastic stand awkwardly placed against a corner in his bedroom.

Such a bachelor pad.

"I like it like that," he says.

"Shut up," I reply. "As if you do. I bet you're just lazy."

"I'm not lazy."

"Excuse me, but one single chair in your living room? No table? What's that? You need more than a chair and a bed to make a house, you know."

"Alright then."

I fidget against his body. I like how his arm wraps around my shoulder. He moves it in tighter as I make myself comfortable. I feel secure, protected, just like I did when he saved me from that customer.

I close my eyes and bask in this glow. It's the best I've felt for a long, long time.

I could stay here like this for days.

"I'm scared, Bay," he says softly under his breath.

My eyes flicker open.

What?

"Scared?"

"I'm scared of the restaurant failing."

"It won't."

"It might. I'm worried it'll collapse, and then I'll be done for."

"What do you mean?"

"I'll lose the respect of my family."

"No, you won't."

He chuckles. "You don't know my parents or my uncle.

Losing this will be another tally of my failures dating back years. I've failed all through my twenties, Bay."

"I doubt it."

"I did. I've spent years screwing all through Europe, wasting days on booze and women. Rockpool failing will just be another one in that long list of my cock-ups."

I sigh and kiss his warm chest in reassurance. I don't like him talking like this about himself. "I'm sure it's not as bad as you're making it out to be."

"No. It's worst," Cliff replies. He pauses. "I proposed to my girlfriend a few months ago, and that backfired. It backfired massively. That's why I'm back here, so focused on this restaurant. In my family's eyes, I fucked up when she rejected me, and now Rockpool's all I have left to prove to them I'm not just a giant failure."

"You're not, though," I reply. "If anyone's the failure around here, it's me. I've worked endless dead-end jobs, never progressing throughout my entire adult life so far. I've tried to start my own business – that day at the bank – but I was rejected. My one dream in life and that was taken away from me. I look back at everything and know I've done nothing. My brother's gone and had a family and is working whilst overcoming the grief of his wife's passing. He's done a lot more than I have. I look back and have nothing to show for myself."

I let out another sigh.

I don't know why I said all that.

I don't know why I blurted that all out to Cliff.

I hope he doesn't get weirded out by me.

Cliff pauses again, digesting what I've said. When he does eventually speak, it's with a quiet firmness.

"It seems like we both need each other, Bay."

My heart leaps at his statement. He says it so casually, like it's a simple fact.

"Why?"

"We both need Rockpool to survive, so how about let's act as a team?"

"What?"

"Let's do this together."

"What are you saying?" I ask, lifting my head so that I can look into his eyes.

"How about we reopen Rockpool together, Bay? Make it new. You and I do it, not as waitress and boss, but as business partners."

Partners?

I bite my lip. His brown eyes stare back at me, full of genuine inquisition. He's waiting for my answer.

He wants us to work together? He wants me to use my skills? Save the restaurant he loves?

I think he really likes me.

"Sure," I reply. "Let's do it. As partners."

21

CLIFF

"How about we go surfing?"

Bay frowns at me. "Surfing?" she asks hesitatingly.

"Yeah, surfing," I reply, gesturing outside my bedroom window towards the clear blue ocean. The late afternoon sun glistens on the waves. "I mean, the ocean is right there. We might as well go in."

"I've never been surfing," Bay replies with a sigh.

I sit up in bed, making Bay turn over. She was snuggled tightly against me until I decided to move. "You've never been surfing?"

"No."

"Never?"

"Nope."

"Have you ever been in the ocean?"

She shrugs. "A couple of times."

"Too much of a city girl, I bet."

Bay rolls her eyes. "Yeah, that's it."

"You need to be broken into the beach life."

She snorts. "*Broken* into the beach life. You mean like a horse?"

"Yeah, kind of like that."

"Right."

I shrug. "Come and see. I'll show you surfing."

Bay turns to me, her big green eyes staring inquisitively back at me. "Okay, sure. Take me out, Cliff."

"Oh, I will."

I find two wetsuits. I give Bay the old one of mine, back when I was a bit skinnier, but the thing still looks massive on her. I laugh at the sight of her in the baggy swimwear and she sternly glares back at me, very much not amused.

"What?" she asks.

"You."

"What about me?"

I smile. "You're cute."

Her cheeks flush and she turns away from me. "Shut up, Cliff," she replies.

I grab one of my surfboards propped up against the unpainted wall in my living room and guide Bay out of the backyard door, across the lawn, and to the beach. She follows me warily.

She thinks I'm out to embarrass her or something. No, I just want to show her the ocean.

The sun is setting over the horizon, and the ocean is bathed in a golden evening glow.

"It looks beautiful," Bay remarks when we reach the white sand of the beach.

I deeply breathe in the cool air whipping off the water, filling my lungs with the fresh, salty breeze. "It is beautiful. This is my favorite time of day," I reply.

Bay smiles and reaches out to take my hand in hers as

we stare out across the blue water. It's just us, the soft breeze, the sun, and the ocean.

It really is beautiful.

Made even better - *perfect* - because Bay Dover is here.

I can't believe Bay and I just had sex. It all felt so *natural*. So right. Her body responded to my light touch, and I found myself wanting her more and more with each passing moment. She was intoxicating to me. I wanted to drink her up. I was *hungry* for her.

I loved the look in her eyes when I revealed my naked body to her, the way she scanned over my muscles and my cock. Her eyes turned me on and lured me to ravish her. It was a feeling I've never had before with a girl, deeper than arousal. Something approaching *love*.

No, stop that, Cliff.

Anything but love.

I was so afraid of what she'll say when I admitted how intimidated I was by her when I told her I like her. It felt like that Paris hotel room, putting my heart out in that proposal to only get rejected.

But it wasn't like that at all.

Bay said she likes me too.

And, at that moment, my heart stopped.

Look at me, the guy who's broken a hundred hearts, brought to his knees by a waitress.

I can't believe it, but here I am, standing in front of the ocean holding Bay Dover's hand.

And really liking it.

Could this moment be any more perfect?

Turns out it can be. In one movement, I take her head in my hands, lean down, and kiss her passionately. She melts into my embrace, and I hang on to hers so that she doesn't disappear. Our lips lock like they're meant to. Like they were always waiting for this moment, traveling to meet right here, right now.

I want to consume her.

I grip her hand tight and lead her into the ocean.

And I teach this city girl to surf.

22

BAY

"Okay, how about we have those hanging lights closer to the front, then?" I ask the builder.

He crosses his arms and raises an eyebrow at my comment. "Closer to the front?"

"Yeah," I say as I take a step forward to stand next to Rockpool's front door. "How about above here? I think they will work here, don't you?"

The builder nods, finally understanding my point. "Actually, that might work."

I scan my eyes over the rest of the ceiling inside Rockpool, looking for any other alternatives for the hanging lights.

No, here seems best.

Suddenly, Pearl and Davy appear at my legs, playing. Davy is chasing Pearl around the restaurant. She giggles with every step as her brother eventually catches up to her.

"Hey, guys," I say after them. "How about you stop running around?"

"But we're bored," Davy replies. "How long do we have to be here?"

I point to the bar. "Maybe you can help with the painting over there?"

They don't need any more encouragement. Pearl and Davy dash over to the painting being done on the bar and eagerly beg to help. The painter laughs and hands them both a small brush, tiny enough not to do too much damage. No one can resist Pearl's cute charms, not even the bunch of rough builders and construction crew I've hired to re-do Rockpool.

Brainstorming plans for the place the other day, Cliff charged me with renovating the restaurant ahead of its big re-opening. Well, more like I *begged* him to renovate the place. It can really do with a makeover. Cliff has no interest in fixing up the inside of the restaurant and, judging from his bachelor pad, he shouldn't go anywhere near interior design, so it all fell to me.

And I'm relishing it.

I'm treating Rockpool like my own business, and am pouring my heart and soul into this project. It helps that Cliff's stuck to his word and is treating me like a true business partner. All the things I've longed to do, what I've dreamed about in running a business all these years, I can finally apply to this restaurant.

I don't want to brag, but Rockpool's going to be a thousand times better when I'm through with it. I've spent the last few days tied up in here, making sure it's going to be perfect. I've spent all my time in here for the past couple of days, barely sleeping, completely focused on realizing my dream for Rockpool.

The front door of the restaurant opens, and Cliff steps inside. He's wearing a suit and looking handsome, as always.

Typical Cliff Finn.

"Hello, Cliff," I mutter. I watch him enter with his cocky walk and charming smile. His presence still makes my heart flutter.

He takes in the restaurant and all the construction going on, noticing the changes I've already made to the place.

"What do you think?" I ask him.

"Wow," he whispers. "You're really doing something here, Bay."

"You like it?"

He winks at me. "We'll see if I do. When you're finished with it."

"Oh, *really*? When I'm finished with it?"

"Yeah, it's too early to tell."

"Well, I'm certainly not finished yet, but I think you're going to be overjoyed with my results."

He takes a step towards me, eyes glinting. "Oh, really? You think?"

"Certainly."

And then he kisses me. I still can't get over it. I can't get over his full lips and the way they make me feel. My mind goes back over the last few days, the happiest days of my life. Cliff's been so kind, but not only that, his body has been exhilarating to me. We've fucked like we've been starved of it, and only the touch of each other can break our thirst. He's found ways of pleasuring me that I've never thought possible. His touch melts me into him.

And I know I've affected him as well. I see bewilderment and untapped desire in his eyes when he fucks me. He's as confused about this newfound lust as I am, but he is also reveling in it as much as me.

We're perfect for each other.

Cliff breaks our kiss and smiles at me. He's so tall, so overbearing. He's my entire world. "I've booked the re-opening for three days from now. Is that enough to get this ready?"

I glance around the room, thinking about the plans and designs I've come up with the builder. All the things we have to get done. "Yeah, we'll be alright. We'll just push hard and get this all done before then. I think it's possible."

"I hope so. There's going to be food critics from all over the country flying into New Water just for this."

"Jesus."

"You sure we'll be ready?"

I hope so.

I'll be confident for him.

"Sure. We'll just have to work extra hard."

"Good."

The restaurant doors swing open again and, just on time, my brother arrives. I've asked him to come. He works in construction and will be able to help me out with this renovation.

"Fisher," I greet.

My brother strolls over to us, nodding at the handiwork of the builders.

"Looking good, sis."

I wave at Cliff. "Fisher, this is Cliff Finn. Cliff, this is my brother."

The two men shake hands, and I see Fisher eyeing up my tall muscular boss, doing the dutiful older brother assessment. I roll my eyes. I'm not in some Regency costume drama; I don't need my brother to duel for my honor or anything. But it is kinda sweet how Fisher is looking out for me. I know he wants only the best.

"Nice to meet you, Cliff."

"Nice to meet you, too."

There's a charged male atmosphere in the air. The kind that only exists when your brother meets the man you're fucking for the first time, and you know they'll either be best friends or lifelong enemies.

I hope they'll be the former.

"Okay, Fisher, I'll like to hear what you think of my designs," I say, taking his shoulder to guide him towards the manager's office.

Cliff shakes his head. "Bay," he says. "You've been here all day and you need a break. I'll take you home and cook you dinner."

"No," I reply. "I can't, Cliff. I can't take a break now with all this work to do. Plus, I have to look after the kids."

Fisher laughs and brushes my hand off his shoulder. "I can look after Pearl and Davy."

"What?"

"I can."

"You sure?"

"I am their dad, Bay. I think I can manage."

"Right. Of course."

"And I can take over here," he says, winking. "Go and have a good evening with Cliff."

"You're absolutely sure? You don't need me?"

My brother chuckles. "I'm positive, Bay. Stop worrying, everything's fine. I'll take control of things from here. Go and have fun, you two."

Fisher practically pushes Cliff and me out of the restaurant, laughing at my concerns.

"Your brother's good to you," Cliff says once we're out on the street.

"He loves me too much, I think," I say as a way of explanation.

"You do need a break," Cliff replies. Then he leans in close to my ear and whispers. "And I do need you in my bed."

Well, how can I say no to that?

23

CLIFF

My erection throbs as I kiss her inner thigh. I slowly close my lips around her warm skin like I'm sucking at her. I want her. I want her flesh.

I continue kissing her skin as I gradually move in closer, getting closer to her wet pussy. Bay gasps as my fingers caress her outer sex, feeling it. Touching it. I like how her body responds to the tips of my fingers as I delicately worm them over her inviting pussy.

Oh, I want her so much.

And I know she wants me to.

But she's going to have to wait. I'm going to bring her to the brink of climax before I'm even thinking of penetrating her with my stiff cock. She's going to have to *beg* for it before I grant her that release. I want to see her moan even more than she's currently doing. I want to see her *squirm*.

My eager mouth finds its way to the tip of her pussy, and now I'm *really* turned on.

We're lying in my bed in my house, both full of the dinner I've cooked for her and a little drunk from the delicious red wine we drank. It was nothing special I made her. I bet she could do a lot better herself. But I wanted to cook for her. I wanted to make her feel special.

Make her know how much she's made me feel in just the last few days.

I smile as I softly bite her clit, savoring her hot taste. Bay gasps again and reaches down to pull at my hair. I like how she does that, how she can't contain herself around me. All her civil manners drop away and unleashed is an unabetted desire for me.

For my cock.

Yes.

I gently flick my tongue over her clit as I push my fingers deep inside her wet opening. She gasps again and her grip around my hair tightens. She really can't contain herself, or her pleasure, any longer.

She's mine. All mine.

I raise my face away from her soft pussy and smile again. "Do you want me, Bay?"

She moans that I've pulled away from her. She wants - *needs* - me against her clit right now. "I want you so much, Cliff. I want you closer. I want you inside me."

"You're gonna have to wait for that, sweetheart. You're gonna have to beg."

"Please, Cliff. Please."

"Nope."

My lips reconnect with her wet pussy and I drive my tongue around her clit, playing with it as she satisfyingly moans again. All the breath in her body springs out and she is breathless.

Breathless over me.

I pump harder with my fingers inside her pussy as she shakes, flicking my fingers in rhythm to her body's rising pleasure.

This is always my favorite bit.

She gasps again, and now I know it's time.

I pull away, and Bay immediately groans and reaches out for me to return, but I playfully swat her hands away. I'm in charge here. She has to submit to what I want, what I want her to feel.

"Flip over," I command, and she does. She obeys me like she should.

She exhales, excited about what may happen next. "What do you want me to do?" she asks.

I lean forward so that my lips press against her ear. With my left hand, I grab a handful of her hair, in complete control over her now. "I'm going to spank you. Punish you."

"Yes," she moans, elation rising in her voice. She *wants* this. "Punish me."

She perks her ass invitingly in the air, practically *begging* for my hand.

And I deliver.

SMACK.

My right hand connects with her exposed asscheek with a resounding spank. Bay whimpers in ecstasy at the punishment.

SMACK.

Again, I spank her ass.

SMACK.

Again.

SMACK.

And again.

Bay *loves* this. She gasps with each spank, titillated beyond belief.

"I like to punish you," I tell her in a deep voice.

"I need it," she replies.

Her asscheek is slightly red from my handprint. She wriggles it in the air, knowing how much her pear-shaped ass *turns* me on.

It turns me so on that I can no longer control myself anymore.

I reach behind me for my condom packet and slide it on over my engorged member. Bay's eyes widen in hopeful excitement. I've brought her to the cusp, but now I'm going to go the full way and penetrate her, and she knows it.

And she wants it.

I aim my cock over her pussy, feeling her get wet by her own juices.

And then I push in.

Bay moans loudly as she accepts me inside her. It's just what I'm hoping for, that delicious first response to my massive cock. I feel her body adapting to it, squeezing around it as I slide inside. I lean over Bay and begin passionately kissing her neck, biting at it like a vampire. She loves this. Her hands trace down my back, scratching at it in a sign of her pleasure.

Now I start to thrust. Bay reacts strongly, crying out breathlessly in my ear.

"You want me?" I ask, whispering against her neck.

"Yes, please. Keep going," she says. "I want you to cum."

Her words spurn me on, and I speed up my thrusts inside her. I feel her.

I feel all of her.

Bay groans again.

My thoughts are dominated by her. By the softness of her skin, by the thickness of her lips. By the shape of her ass and tits. By the warmth of her pussy.

I fuck her hard, and I don't stop until we both cum.

* * *

We lie in bed. Bay cozies up to me, warm under my sheets. The post-sex bliss. I lie back and close my eyes in utter relaxation.

This is where I should be.

Bay has been so good to me. We started off as foes, but we've ended up as business partners.

And I feel safe around her.

The last time I did care about someone, they threw it back in my face. Rejected me. The last time I cared about someone, I was left on my knees in a Paris hotel room alone wondering what I've done wrong.

I closed myself up then, fearing to be hurt like that again. I knew I couldn't endure another round like that. It was worse than any physical pain I've felt.

Has Bay Dover really melted my cold heart?

Maybe she has.

I just hope it stays like this. I hope my heart remains unbroken. I hope I'm not left on my knees again. Alone and shattered.

I hope Rockpool survives and thrives. I hope it doesn't collapse.

But there's something I haven't told Bay. I haven't told her that I am prepared to sell it if it all goes bad, that I'm ready to walk away from it all. I would much prefer selling the restaurant than seeing it crumble. Bay would never understand if I let her in on this. She doesn't know what it's like to be pressured by a rich family.

I will sell Rockpool before it falls apart. I can't fail. Not with it. Not again like that Paris hotel room. I can't afford to fail again in front of my family. They've seen me fail with Cleo Dash; they can't see me fail with Rockpool as well.

I feel Bay slowly drift off to sleep on my arm. Her soft purring as she falls unconscious.

I don't want to lose Rockpool.

And, most of all, I don't want to lose Bay.

24

BAY

IT'S NIGHT.

I slip out of Cliff's tight embrace of his muscular arm and slide down the bed, careful not to wake him. Getting off the bed, I step onto his hoodie. The fabric is soft on my toes.

Ah, so that's where it is.

Bingo.

I lean down to pick up the hoodie, fitting it over my head. I'm as silent as I can be to not stir Cliff. I turn my head to check back on him. He lies so peacefully in bed, his defined chest slowly rising and falling with his breath.

I can't believe I've been sleeping next to him.

Sex with him is out-of-this-world insane. I still feel it in my body hours after we've climaxed. The man *knows* what to do to please me, and I love him for it.

With Cliff's hoodie on, way too over-sized for me, I sneak out of his room, trying hard not to make a sound. I cautiously make my way into the kitchen and living space, wrapping my arms around me in an effort for my body temperature to stay above freezing.

I head straight for his fridge. Of course. The light from it illuminates the kitchen in a warm glow. I scan the shelves until I find the cheese platter.

Bingo again.

I take the platter out and start nibbling at the expensive cheese, content that I've found what I've been craving for. What a great midnight snack.

I bring the cheese out onto the backyard, sitting on one of the chairs outside. I stare out across the ocean and eat the food like the rat I am, watching the waves as they curl and fall onto the sandy shores.

New Water's a beautiful place.

I'm happy I've moved here. I'm happy I've found the job at Rockpool.

I'm happy I've met Cliff.

I think I like him.

Like, really like him.

But, going from past experience, I know that isn't going to help things. Not for me. There's a reason why guys I've liked have never properly asked me out, and that's simply because I'm not as pretty as other girls. Especially the kind of girls I know Cliff's been with. Girls like that Cleo Dash. Supermodels. Actresses.

It's not some fake modesty, I just know I'm a bit of a plain jane, and I'm okay with that. It's just that I always fall for a guy like Cliff. The unobtainable one. The one who just, in the words of my friend-slash-serial-dater back in Melbourne, likes to *fuck and dump* girls like me. We're easy because we fall in love too quickly with a gorgeous face and a winning smile. We're not the relationship girls, we're the ones to have some fun with, to have a brief fling with, and then discard.

And maybe Cliff is just like that. Judging by his reputation, he *is* that guy. The one with the gorgeous face and winning smile who's charmed his way through half of Europe, and I'm just another one in a long list of conquests. Just another girl.

I wrap my arms around me again, feeling the soft cotton of his hoodie against my chin. It even smells of him. Expensive shower gel and that nice European aftershave he wears. I breathe him in and sigh.

I don't want to be just another girl.

But I'm ready to resign myself to that fact.

There'll always be another Cleo Dash. I'm just a waitress who'll be fun for a few weeks.

Then he'll let me go.

Just like every other guy.

I just like him, that's all.

I'll just enjoy this moment and let him go when the time's right. When he runs off.

But I know I'll get my heart broken. It's too late for me.

I like him.

It's too late for me for this to be clean and swift.

I'll be heartbroken over Cliff Finn and I know it.

I hear the glass door slide open behind me and I turn to see Cliff stepping out into the night air. He's completely naked, but he doesn't seem to care. His old cocky confidence. No one else can see him out here but me. It's just Cliff, the waves, his naked body, and me.

No matter what light I see him in, he's utterly *gorgeous*.

"What are you doing out here, Bay?" he asks, bleary-eyed.

I lift up the half-eaten cheese platter in response, shrugging.

I'm guilty as charged.

"Oh," he replies, smiling. "You're very cute."

"And you're beautiful," I say.

"Shut up, you." Cliff strolls over and embraces me in a tight hug from behind. "What are you doing with my hoodie? That's mine."

"It's mine now," I snigger, and Cliff kisses me on the cheek.

"Yeah, you're very cute," he says.

"Now it's your turn to shut up."

"How was your break, Miss Dover?"

"Even better because you were there," I reply.

"Oh, I know."

"But I need to get back to work in the morning. I can't spend too long away from Rockpool. Everything has to be *just right* for the re-opening."

"Just relax, Bay. Just let me hug you. Everything will be alright."

At his urging, I lean back into his embrace, but my mind still races.

I hope everything will be alright.

Even though I know he'll let me go someday soon, I just can't resist him. I can't stop my heart from falling from him. I know it's wrong, but it feels so right.

Sitting out here with Cliff's arms around me, the waves crashing and the night sky twinkling with stars, I feel protected. Safe.

I never want this to end.

But I know it will.

25

BAY

I PUFF as I scan through the documents laid out on the desk, my cheeks bulging as I let out built-up air in my lungs. I'm sitting in the manager's office at Rockpool, checking over everything before the big re-opening this time tomorrow night.

And I'm nervous.

I have to make everything perfect; there can't be any mistakes here. Rockpool has to survive. It has to make money. I can't afford to screw this up. This is important.

And I'm freaking out.

I re-check the documents again, quickly skipping through the pages. Everything seems alright, but I can't be too certain. Just a few little things to tweak in the morning and we should be all set for the grand re-opening in the night.

Fingers crossed.

There's a knock on the door and Cliff walks in with a

smile on his face and a glass of red wine in his hand, his favorite drink.

"How's it going?" he asks.

"Hm," I grunt in reply.

Cliff hands me the glass of wine. "Maybe this might help."

I take a sip, enjoying the strong dry taste. I hand the glass back to him. "Thanks."

Cliff sits down beside me and takes out his laptop. He boots it up to show Rockpool's financial records, and he scrolls through them, reading. I watch him as he checks each page with his intense stare, ticking off the individual numbers as he scans through them.

He's so *freaking* gorgeous. His square jaw, black, slightly curly hair, and deep brown eyes are shining from the laptop screen's glare. His skin is tanned and flawless. He's just so incredibly *beautiful*.

What a man.

I reach out and steal the glass back off him, drinking a large gulp before he can protest. I need that wine when I'm sitting so close to him and unable to contain myself from lashing out and getting him to fuck me right here and now. I need the wine to calm my nerves about sitting right next to Superman.

But, despite how much I really, really want to, we can't have sex. Not now. Not while I still need to double-check everything for tomorrow. Not while Cliff scrolls through the restaurant's financial records.

I turn back to my documents. I pull out the new menu we've printed off and I go through it line-by-line. I check each word.

And then I see it.

"Cliff," I say. "How do you spell Lemon Posset?"

He looks up at me from the laptop screen. "Posset? As in *p-o-s-s-e-t?*"

"One T?"

"Yeah."

"You sure it's spelled with one T?"

"I'm sure. Why are you asking?"

Well, that's not what he's written here.

I lower my gaze so that I appear as a berating schoolteacher, glaring at Cliff like he's a naughty schoolboy. "Then why have you written it with two Ts?"

"Let me have a look." He snatches the menu off me and scans through it. I watch his eyes flicker across the words. "Oh, shit."

"Yes. Shit."

Cliff shrugs. "Who'll notice?"

"I'm guessing all those food critics you're inviting, that's who."

"If we lose a star because we misspelled posset, then they're just being pedantic."

I sigh. "That's not it, Cliff. Everything just has to be *perfect.* Don't you get it?"

His lips form into a wide smirk. "I do get it."

I playfully punch him on the shoulder. "Can you just be serious for a moment, Cliff?"

"Oh, I am serious." Cliff reaches over and takes my head in his hands. And then he kisses me deeply. I lose myself in his touch, unable to keep up my anger at his spelling mistake when he's so goddamn gorgeous. Not when he's so goddamn good at kissing.

"This is serious," I repeat, breaking off from his kiss. "We need to make sure everything's good for tomorrow. We can't afford any mistakes."

"How about you forget all about this for the night? I'm

sure everything's good. You've been at this for the last few days practically twenty-four-seven."

He's right, but there's a reason why I'm working so hard.

I can't afford to lose this job.

I can't afford to lose Cliff Finn.

"No, I can't let this be," I say. Cliff reaches back over and starts kissing my neck tenderly. I gasp at his lips touching my exposed neck. His lips on my skin make my body hot, but I try to power through. "I have to keep working until the party to make sure everything's ready."

I can't give in to temptation. Not now.

"Stop for the night," Cliff moans as he continues kissing my neck. My hand grabs the back of his head to try to stop him, but it's a feeble attempt, and he easily swats me away. He is biting at my flesh like he's consuming me. I gasp again as his mouth nears my ear. He begins nibbling at my earlobe and I feel so bright inside. His lips are wet with the red wine, and I know he's leaving a dark red trail up along my skin as he ravishes me.

"I... can't do this... gotta keep... working."

But it's useless trying to resist him. I embrace his touch. His lips. His wandering hands as they circle my breasts greedily. I moan when his fingers squeeze my erect nipples, when he forcefully grabs my tits in each hand.

"Admit it, Bay," Cliff whispers. "You want this."

"I do," I breathlessly say, shivering at his touch. "I want this. And I want you."

Cliff stands up and, without a warning, picks my entire body up in one go. He lifts me into his arms and carries me out of the manager's office, careful not to bang my head on the doorframe on the way out, and he takes me into Rockpool's kitchen. I giggle in excitement as his muscular body treats me like nothing. He carries me like I weigh no more than that glass of red wine he brought into the office. He takes me right into the kitchen and lays me against the main counter. I open my lips to breathe in after the surprise of being taken like that, but before I can do anything, his lips are around mine and I'm sucking him in totally.

His hands reach down and part my legs, his fingers strong against my thighs.

He can do whatever he wants with me.

Whatever.

He.

Wants.

I'm all his.

26

BAY

I'M STILL in the manager's office when Cliff's phone rings. When it does, both of us jump in our seats, surprised by the loud intrusion whilst we work on the finishing touches before the re-opening party.

"It's Cove and Ripley," he says, checking his phone. "They're outside."

Cliff's cousin and his wife are the first to arrive at the restaurant.

He heads to the door to let them in and I stand just outside the manager's office, nervous. The last time I met Cliff's family was on my first day at Rockpool, when I screwed up their order. They probably think me rude, or at least incompetent.

I wonder what Cliff's told them about me, or whether he has at all.

I scratch at my arm as Cliff unlocks the front door and brings them inside.

It's still an hour or so before the party's meant to start,

and I'm still finishing printing off all the menus and making sure everything in the kitchen is up to scratch. We've hired some temporary chefs to work in there whilst I attend the re-opening, but next week it'll be me in there amongst the pans and grills.

If tonight goes well.

If everything works out.

Cliff warmly greets his cousin and his wife, then brings them over to me, smiling broadly. I smile back, still so incredibly anxious.

It's his surfer cousin, Cove, and the American girl.

"This is Cove and Ripley," Cliff says, introducing us. "This is Bay."

"Right, Bay," Ripley replies with her nice American accent. "It's good to put a name to a face."

"Hi," I reply, my anxiousness betrayed in my voice.

Bay smiles. "If I remember right, you weren't that keen on introducing us the other night, Cliff."

"The other night was... something *different*," Cliff tries to explain, his eyes widening as he fumbles for words. Ripley winks at me as he struggles to speak, happy to put him on the spot like this.

I must admit, I like it too.

"Nice to meet you, Bay," Cove says, offering to shake my hand. His arm is as muscular as Cliff's. Their athletic frame and popping biceps clearly run in the family. "Cliff's told me *all* about you."

My eyebrows raise at Cliff. "Has he now?"

Cliff anxiously laughs it off and brushes Cove away. "No, I haven't."

Has he actually?

"Yes, you have. All you've been doing is talking non-stop about the pretty new waitress."

Non-stop?

"Okay," Cliff chuckles, shaking his head in embarrassment. "That's enough. How about we get a drink at the bar, Cove?"

"See you later," Cliff's cousin says to me, smiling a dazzling white smile that runs in the Finn family as he follows Cliff further down the restaurant.

I'm left with Ripley, the brown-hair Natalie Portman-lookalike.

"He's not lying though," she says. "Cliff has been talking about you pretty much all the time."

"Oh, God. I can't begin to imagine what he's said."

"Don't worry," she says, placing her arm on mine in a joking reassurance. "It's all good."

"Good. I don't want to be the center of any silly rumors."

"Well, you've caused quite a stir, Bay."

"A stir? How?"

"It's a rare person to tame a Finn, especially someone like Cliff."

I snort at her comment. I can't believe it. Me? Cliff? Tamed? "I haven't *tamed* him," I reply.

"You sure? He seems much happier with you than he has at any time since I've known him, including when he dated that supermodel."

"You mean Cleo Dash?"

Ripley rolls her eyes at the name. "Ah. So, you've heard about that?"

"Yeah, he told me about her."

"Well, he's kept that a pretty close secret from everyone else, including his own family."

"Yeah?"

"He doesn't talk about it, not at all with any of us."

"Really?"

"But he's told you," Ripley replies with a smirk. "See, as

I said. *Tamed.*"

I laugh again. I like this American girl. She's sassy and witty, with a clever glint in her eye. She's smarter than she lets on. "I don't think *Tamed* is the word I would use."

"Trust me, I've been in your position before with a Finn boy. I know a fellow lion-tamer when I see one."

"Ha."

I *really* like her.

"How about a drink?" I ask. "Away from the boys. I keep a very nice bottle of wine hidden in the kitchen if you'd like a glass."

Ripley clasps her hands together in joy. I think she likes wine as much as I do. "Oh, I'd love to."

* * *

We spend the next hour happily gossiping together in the kitchen, surrounded by the chefs putting the finishing touches on the party food. We sit up on the kitchen counter, sharing my secret bottle of wine. The alcohol flows freely and so do our lips full of talk.

"I haven't told Cliff about this," I say, gesturing at my stash of good wine.

Ripley's eyes light up as she spins her glass around, observing the liquid swivel. "Don't worry, I'll keep it between us. It's our little secret."

I take a big sip from my own glass. "So, Cliff tells me you're a nurse. What made you come to Australia? What made you come all the way to New Water, of all places?"

Ripley nods in the direction of the bar. "Him."

"Ah, I see."

"You know, I hated Cove at first. I thought he was a right dick."

"That's what I thought of Cliff at first."

"It's the Finn men. First impressions are always wrong when it comes to them."

I chuckle. "You're telling me."

"But after a while, Cove showed his true side. It was like I had to crack away bricks surrounding him, if you know what I mean."

"I think I do."

"It took some time but, before I knew it, there I was, standing on a beach, knowing in my heart that I love this man," Ripley says. She shakes her head. "It sounds crazy, I know. I probably sound like a total nutcase."

"Trust me," I reply, taking her hand. "After the week I've just had with Cliff, you don't sound crazy at all."

* * *

SOON THE OTHER guests start to arrive. Ripley and I, swaying from being a little bit *too* tipsy, stagger out of the kitchen and into the main part of the restaurant. We stand by the front door with Cliff and Cove, welcoming people into Rockpool. Famous food critics Cliff's shown me pictures of swan in to the restaurant. I recognize them, and I make the effort to smile and chat. It's not easy for me to be this sociable, but Rockpool's future hangs on it, and so I force myself to work hard. This whole networking thing comes easy to Cliff, unlike me. He's an extrovert when it comes to this stuff, and I guess going to elite private schools gives you that easy confidence and swagger to excel in social situations like these.

Cliff's other cousin, Sandy, and her husband, Skipper, soon arrive. I also recognize them from the other night. Sandy was the beautiful blonde woman who told me she'd deal with Cliff. I bet she did. There's a tough steeliness under her pretty blonde exterior. Cove and Ripley warmly greet them, and I am reintroduced, still completely anxious. Sandy puts me at ease with her classic Finn smile and a secret joke about Cliff she shares between us, whispering into my ear so that her cousin can't hear.

"He used to be scared of the dark when he was a kid. Like, *really* scared."

"What are you saying?" Cliff asks his cousin with a nervous expression.

"Nothing," I reply with a wink back at Sandy. "She's told me nothing."

"I don't trust her. Bay, don't listen to a word she says. She's the devil."

With most of the guests having arrived and filling out the restaurant, Ripley pulls me away from the crowd towards the back of the room.

"I thought you might want a moment to breathe," she says to me as we clutch our wine glasses against the wall.

"Thank you," I whisper. She must've seen how overwhelmed I was getting with all the people at the front door. Even though I helped him put this all together, this is still Cliff's restaurant. He deserves the spotlight. Plus, he's much better than I am at dealing with all the important food critics and Australian celebrities that have turned up.

The crowd mingles around us, all standing. Eating from canapes boards and drinking expensive Australian vintage wine.

"Let's cheers to Rockpool," Ripley says, raising her glass. I smile and chink mine against hers. "This is as much your day as it is Cliff's. I know he didn't redesign this place. He doesn't have the talent."

"Well, I don't want to brag, but most of the decisions were mine," I smugly reply, causing her to laugh.

"I think, Bay, that this is the start of a beautiful friendship," Ripley says.

"Me too."

There's a loud commotion in front of us. Ripley and I strain our necks, trying to see what's going on.

Everyone's talking to Cliff.

Calling him to do a speech.

He stands up on top of one of the restaurant tables, hands raised, and with a big smile on his face. The man looks gorgeous in any situation. The crowd quiets down and people stop eating and drinking to listen to what he's going to say.

"Welcome, everyone," Cliff starts, his voice booming around the hushed restaurant. "Welcome to the re-opening of Rockpool."

Everyone applauds. Ripley looks at me and smiles.

"This is the start of a new adventure in my life," Cliff continues. "A new chapter for Rockpool and for New Water. Finally, a decent restaurant in the center of town. As many of our regulars can see, we've made some major adjustments to the place. A complete re-haul of our menu and a re-design of our restaurant. We shall be opening better than ever."

There's another scatter of applause. Cliff waits for it to die down before he resumes his speech.

"We've been very busy the last few days. There's been a crazy amount of work to do. I must, therefore, acknowledge the work of Miss Dover in being the talent behind all this."

Cliff gestures towards me and starts another round of clapping. Everyone's eyes turn towards me, curious about this strange girl Cliff has mentioned. I blush, uneasy with the attention. I raise my glass in thanks to Cliff and divert my eyes to the ground. I wish the spotlight's soon taken off me.

He's sweet for thanking me, though.

I knew he didn't have to.

I make eye contact with Cliff and he winks at me, knowing what he's doing. The cheeky bastard.

It's still incredibly sweet.

"Now, let me talk about what new menu items we've put together for you to sample today," Cliff says, redirecting all the room's attention back onto him. "There are a few things I'll like to go through..."

He's interrupted by the restaurant's front door opening. Everyone's attention quickly turns to the person stepping in. The woman walking in is tall, blonde, and very slim. Like a supermodel.

I think I recognize her.

Cliff's eyes widen as she walks into the crowded restaurant. His face transforms into one of shock.

Something's wrong. He knows this girl. He's surprised by her being here.

"I think that's enough, everyone," he says hesitatingly, still fixated by the new arrival. He's cut his speech short. "Why carry on talking when we can eat, drink, and be merry?"

Cliff disappears off the table and into the crowd, and I am left staring at the new beautiful woman who's just walked in.

I know her.

Ripley gasps and whispers to me, confirming my worst fears. But I don't need her to tell me who that woman is. Even she's shocked by this arrival. "That's her," she says, breathless. "That's Cleo Dash."

Cliff's ex.

27

CLIFF

CLEO DASH.

She's here.

She's come to the restaurant.

It wasn't a trick of the light, or a hallucination, or anything supernatural. I *saw* Cleo Dash enter Rockpool just then. I can recognize that face anywhere. The blonde hair. Her angular features. It was her. For sure.

She's here.

I turn and leave the restaurant out the side emergency exit, faking to some guests eager for a chat that I needed a moment on my own after the speech. I immediately make my way around to the back of the building to the trash area where we keep the restaurant bins for collection, desperate to get away from everyone. Desperate to get away from *her*.

Cleo Dash is here.

I lean against the wall and recover my breath. My hands are shaking. My breathing is shallow. I'm in a state of shock.

The last time I saw her was in Paris, in that hotel room.

And now she's stepped through into my restaurant on the other side of the world a few months later, as if it were the most normal thing to do.

She's in there, in my restaurant. Somewhere.

I grip my shirt tightly and undo my top button, needing space.

Why would she come? Why would she travel all the way to New Water?

I thought she'd be in America, getting ready to film that superhero series of hers. Why would she fly halfway across the world? Why does she need to see me?

I hear footsteps approaching. I spin around, faking a smile in case it's one of the guests who've stumbled outside.

It's Cove.

"That was her, wasn't it?" he asks me as he marches over. I quickly check to see if anyone else is following him. Nobody. *Good.*

I want to be alone.

"Yes," I reply and slump up against the restaurant wall, exhausted and still shocked.

"Do you know what she's doing here?" Cove asks.

"No."

"Do you know why she's come? Is it to see you?"

"Cove, I don't know," I reply, rubbing my closed eyes with my fingers. "I don't know why she's here. I don't know what she wants with me."

"Shit, man. This is tough."

I chuckle darkly. "Yeah. It is."

"You're gonna have to find out why she's here in town."

"I don't even want to know. It's not anything good, that's for sure."

"Yeah. I bet it won't be," he says. "So, what are you going to do about it?"

"I don't know," I reply. "Nothing?"

"Yeah?"

I sigh. "But I do want closure. She just walked out on me, man. Maybe she's back to apologize."

"Maybe," Cove replies. "You think so? Is that what she's like?"

"I don't know."

"What will you say if she does apologize?"

I scratch my forehead. "I honestly don't know what I would do. I'm still completely overwhelmed with her walking in like that. Is she in there still?"

Cove shrugs.

"I didn't see her when I left," he says. "She did choose the worst possible time to reappear, though."

"That's Cleo, though. Drama queen. She always knows how to make an entrance."

"Well, she certainly did today."

There's another set of footsteps approaching. Cove and I anxiously check who it is like we're naughty schoolboys smoking and hiding from the teacher at the back of the school.

Bay rounds the corner. Her eyes are wild when she sees us. It's like there's an accusatory look on her face.

"Here's where you both are," she says, glaring at the restaurant's bins surrounding us in disgust.

Yep, I'm here amongst the trash.

Cove glances from her to me. "I'll leave you two alone," he says before striding back into the restaurant.

"That was her?" Bay asks.

I nod. No point in lying to her. "Yes."

"Cleo Dash?"

"Yep."

"Your ex?"

"Yes."

"What's she doing here?"

"That's what Cove, and I were just talking about. I don't know."

Bay crosses her arms and stares at me like she's investigating something. "You didn't know she was coming here?"

"No. Why would I?"

"You didn't ask her to come?"

"Of course, I didn't."

"No?"

"No," I reply. "Bay, I don't like your tone."

"My tone?"

"You're acting like the Spanish Inquisition or something."

"So, you didn't invite her to the re-opening party?"

Wow, she really thinks I've gone behind her back and done this.

It's like there's a gulf between us. This afternoon we were so close, and now, with Cleo turning up like this out of the blue, Bay and I have split apart.

"How many times do I need to say I didn't invite her for you to believe me?" I ask.

"I just don't understand, Cliff. Why would she turn up here? She dumped you. What does she want?"

I raise my hands. "Whoa. I don't know what you're talking about. I didn't invite her. You have to believe me. I don't know what she's doing here."

Bay pauses her tirade. She thinks for a moment, sighs, then slowly nods. "Okay," she says. "I believe you."

"Good."

"Just... please ask her to leave. It's crazy enough re-opening this place without someone like her coming in. I know this makes me out as some paranoid crazy person, but please do it for me. Please ask her to leave."

She's right. Cleo shouldn't be here.

"I'll do it, Bay. For you."

I also want Cleo to leave, but at the same time, I do want the opportunity to speak to her. I want to find out why she's here.

What she wants.

Is she really here to apologize?

What if she wants me back?

What about Bay?

I don't know what to think anymore.

"Thank you, Cliff," Bay says.

"Sure," I reply, but I still feel like there's now an uneasy air between us.

That gulf is stretching further and further wide.

The side door opens, and Cove walks out. My heart races, thinking it might be Cleo, that maybe my cousin is with her.

But no, it's only Cove.

Bay and I both face him expectedly.

"She's gone," Cove says. "Cleo's left the party."

28

BAY

I LOOK at myself in the mirror and tie my hair back, watching myself carefully all the while.

I fit the restaurant apron around my waist. The new logo for Rockpool features prominently on the side of it, a classy black signature. I check myself and my new uniform out in the mirror and nod my head, satisfied.

Ready for my first shift at the newly re-opened Rockpool.

Here goes.

Last night was crazy. The party, overall, seemed to go fine. It seems like everybody enjoyed themselves and liked the food we served. I mean, they drank all the wine, so I'm sure we'll get some very good, and slightly drunk-written reviews in the next few days. Fingers crossed.

But Cleo.

Cleo Dash.

The supermodel-slash-blockbuster actress. She turned up and now she's here. Somewhere. In town.

She crashed the party last night and then disappeared without a trace minutes later.

Cliff reassured me all night that nothing was going on between them, that he had no inkling that she would show up, and I do trust him. I have to trust him.

But still...

I knew, when I first heard about her, that Cleo would factor in at some point, that Cliff and I would have to address her, and the hold she has over his past, at some point in the time we're together. But I would never have guessed in a million years she would turn up, unannounced, at his restaurant in a small town in Australia. I never thought I would ever actually see her in person, and so soon after Cliff and I have hooked up.

But yet, there she was last night, walking into Rockpool looking every inch the beautiful movie starlet she is.

And it drove me crazy.

Are they still together? Does Cliff still have feelings for her?

She broke his heart, but does he still pine for her?

I don't know.

I don't even know what it is that Cliff and I share. Are we together? Are we boyfriend and girlfriend or just some version of fuck buddies? Friends with benefits? Am I just the nearest and easiest girl for Cliff to hang onto for a while before he heads back into his old self?

Am I just another girl to keep his bed warm before he goes back to Cleo Dash?

I don't want to think of him in that way, as some kind of heartless and cruel playboy, but the arrival of Cleo has thrown everything in my head into doubt. With her angular beauty and gorgeous long blonde hair, I don't know what Cliff thinks anymore.

Am I turning into the crazy stalker girlfriend? The creepy and needy one?

Over-attached. Overly paranoid. Scary? Is that who I am?

I realize what it is. I'm *terrified* of Cleo. Of who she is and what she can do if she decides she wants Cliff back.

I will be hopeless.

She's a supermodel. An actress in the biggest blockbuster film franchise out there.

And I am a waitress-turned-amateur chef.

What hope do I have to keep the affections of a bad boy hunk like Cliff Finn?

Why is she back?

What does she want?

And why was Cliff acting so strange when he saw her? He ran away. He didn't want to see her. He was *scared* of seeing her again.

Does she still have a hold over his heart?

Whatever it is, I'm going to find out.

29

CLIFF

THERE'S a knock on the manager's office door. I look up from my desk with a frown.

Who could this be?

It's still too early in the day, a few hours before dinner service, and the restaurant is still closed. I haven't even unlocked the front doors yet, so no customer should be inside yet.

It could be Bay. She might've come early.

Maybe, but she hasn't said she would be.

I drop the papers in front of me. The financial records land on the desk with a thud. Rockpool's in a bad shape, even despite the successful re-opening party, maybe even *because* of it. We've spent so much money this last week, with no returns yet. No profit has yet to come in.

If a miracle doesn't happen soon, then this restaurant is toast.

And by soon, I mean *right now*.

"Come in," I say, and the office door swings open.

And in walks Cleo Dash.

My heart stops at the sight of her beautiful model face, high cheekbones, bright eyes, and luscious blonde hair. It's her.

She's here.

A lump catches in my throat and I stutter.

"Cleo," I say, shocked that she's standing in my office.

I haven't seen her since last night when she walked into the re-opening party unannounced and then promptly disappeared. It was like she was a ghost.

But now she's here, standing in front of me in Rockpool's office, smiling at me with her perfect white teeth.

She looks *beautiful*. It's like she's fresh off the front page of a tabloid magazine. She's ethereal, just like the future movie star she is. A goddess among men.

"Hello, Cliff." Her voice is soft and inviting. A singsong voice like Marilyn Monroe's. Seductive. Her American accent is soft and gentle. The best word to describe her voice would be *cooing*.

And that's what she's doing now.

My heart wants to leap out of my chest as she speaks. I remember why I fell in love with her, why all men who meet her fall in love with her. She's a blonde all-American angel. Silky white skin and full red lips.

She's like a starlet out of 1930s Hollywood, all dazzling and close-up sparkles.

"What are you doing here?" I ask, my own voice trembling and hesitant. I suddenly don't know how to speak clearly. I'm just so enamored with her powerful presence, her *intoxicating* movie star presence.

"What am I doing here? What do you think I'm doing here?"

"I don't know, Cleo."

"Well, Cliff," she says, gliding towards me. She sits on

my desk, leaning over so that we are *incredibly* and uncomfortably close. Our noses are practically touching. "Let me put this bluntly. We both don't have time for games."

"No."

"Let me tell you straight-up." Her eyes light up and she pouts. Her full red lips are inches from mine. "I'm here because I want you back, Cliff."

"What?"

No way.

"How can I make it any clearer? I made a mistake, Cliff, in letting you go."

"Yeah, that was a mistake."

"My mistake," she says, licking her lips. "*Oops*."

"That's why you've come and found me? To tell me you've made a mistake?"

"And I had to travel across the world to do so, Cliff. I knew you'd be here. I have my sources. I knew I'd find you last night."

"That was uncalled-for," I say, but Cleo ignores me and continues.

"When I walked in and saw your face as you looked at me, I knew that there is still that connection between us. I could see it. That connection is something that can't be broken easily, and you know it. You and I are meant to be together, and if it weren't for my little... *mishap* back in Paris, we would still be."

"So?" I ask in disbelief. "You've changed your mind?"

"Yes."

"And you want us to be together?"

"Exactly."

"Cleo, you walked out on me back there in Paris. You disappeared completely from my life; how can I ever forget that?"

Cleo rolls her eyes like I'm repeating myself. Going over

old ground. I know she wants to move past this. "As I said, that was my mistake. But I'm here now. I'm with you now."

I shake my head. "I know you, Cleo. I know there's more to it than that. What is it? Why do you suddenly want me now? What's made you change your mind?"

She crosses her legs and leans in closer. "Ugh, so many questions, Cliff."

"Well, I want answers. You *disappeared*, Cleo."

"Fine," she says, flicking her hair back and staring at me with her piercing eyes. "As you may know, I've been cast in the Vindicator film series as the newest superhero."

I raise my eyebrows. "Congratulations."

"Don't be so snarky, Cliff."

"Oh, I'm not," I reply, snarky. "You always wanted to be even more rich and famous than you were."

"I'll ignore your little digs, Cliff," she says, tracing a perfectly manicured nail seductively across my neck. "As I was saying, I've just been cast in this film series, and the producers and the studio have been all over my back. They don't want me to be single. Apparently, it doesn't fit in with this golden-girl aesthetic they're trying to promote. It hurts sales in China or something."

"You never really were the golden girl."

"Oh, really, you are so *snarky*, Cliff. I expect better from you," Cleo says, biting her lip. It's like my dry sarcasm drips off her with no effect. She's as cold as ice. Like her heart. Like the way she crushed mine with her laugh at my proposal.

She is still so *beautiful*, though.

"So, you've come back to make me your boyfriend because you need to look wholesome for your movie career?"

"Not just because of that."

"What else then?"

She wraps her legs around mine, places her skinny arms over my shoulder, and leans in close so that we are nearly kissing. "I *love* you, Cliff."

"What?" I stammer.

"I love you. That's why I'm back. I made a mistake in Paris."

"I don't understand."

She breathes in sharply. I watch her lips softly part. We could kiss right now. "Well, believe this, Cliff. I've reconsidered, and I say *yes* to your proposal."

"To my proposal?"

"Yes," she replies, tightening her grip around me. "And what about you? Do you say yes?"

The office door opens and in walks someone. Both Cleo and I turn.

It's Bay.

Oh, no.

Her eyes widen.

She's shocked.

Understandably.

Cleo's sitting on my desk, her legs and arms around me. Our mouths are nearly touching.

If I were Bay, I would be very, *very* shocked.

And she most certainly is.

"What's going on?" she asks, her mouth agape, her hand still gripped around the door handle. I don't move, I'm as shocked as Bay is.

Cleo laughs and lifts herself away from me and off the table. She stands between Bay and me like a wall. Aggressively. She doesn't know who Bay is, but her finely tuned instincts tell her that she's a threat. I know Cleo too well. I know she sees Bay as someone to deal with quickly and decisively.

"I've heard there's been problems with this place," Cleo

says, her voice lower and stronger than before. This is all directed at Bay, I know. Cleo glances around the room like she's sizing up Rockpool. Like she's sizing up Bay. "I'm prepared to buy this restaurant off you, Cliff. I've come into quite a bit of money thanks to this movie contract. I'll buy it for you, Cliff. For us."

"What are you talking about?" Bay asks.

"I'll buy it." Cleo snaps her fingers. "*Boom*, no more money problems. No more issues with this place. With my injection of cash, you wouldn't have to ever worry about this place again, Cliff."

Bay's eyes flicker from Cleo to me. "You can't let her buy Rockpool, Cliff," she says. "You can't."

"You want to buy this restaurant?" I ask Cleo.

"Yes. For you, Cliff. No more headache. No more stress."

Bay shakes her head. "You can't buy this place."

Cleo smiles. "Oh, I can. I've got the money, and I've heard about all the problems here. You need money."

"We can manage fine, thank you very much," Bay retorts. "Tell her, Cliff."

But Bay is wrong, and Cleo is right.

I sigh. "I've looked at the numbers, Bay. We need investment. We need money."

Bay's voice is quiet. It breaks my heart. "No, Cliff."

She's wrong. I've seen the financial records. We're going to collapse. We need money.

"I'm sorry, Bay."

"Well, what about your family, Cliff? Can't you borrow money from them?"

I shake my head. "I will never borrow money off them, Bay."

"So, you would rather let Rockpool collapse than borrow money off your own family?"

"Yes," I reply, and Bay's voice shakes in anger.

"I honestly don't understand you, Cliff."

"Rockpool's in bad straits," I explain. "I'll take the money, no matter if it comes from Cleo or someone else, rather than see this place fail."

"And you'll take it from her, but not from your family?"

"Yes," I reply. It's the truth. I will never let my family see me become a failure again. Never.

I'm trying to be reasonable here. Pragmatic.

But Bay doesn't see that. She's got tears in her eyes. They sparkle in the office's lighting. She wells up looking at me, turns her head, and storms outside, out of the office. She disappears as quickly as she appeared.

Cleo turns around with a triumphant smile across her face.

I'm trying to be rational.

Why can't Bay see that?

I need to explain it to her, explain the predicament Rockpool's in.

I launch out of my chair and out of the office, chasing after Bay.

And I hear Cleo laughing behind me.

"She'll be the first to go," she says as I run out of the restaurant in pursuit of Bay.

Not if I can stop this.

30

BAY

WITH ALL MY FORCE, I push open the front doors of Rockpool and storm outside into the hot summer air. I turn right and head straight on down the main street of New Water, away from the restaurant. Towards the beach.

I'm practically sprinting towards the ocean, not caring about anyone in my way. Wet tears stream down my cheeks as I march ahead.

And I don't look back.

I'm still recovering over what just happened, still getting used to what I saw and heard in that office.

Cliff and that Cleo woman embracing, near kissing. The images of her legs draped over him, her perfect ass sitting perkily on his desk, her smile at me as I walked in, and how she reveled in my shock and horror haunt me as I rush down the main street. Cleo Dash doesn't know who I am. She hasn't even met me before, but I bet she could tell how in love I am with Cliff. She could tell how in love I am with a man I could never truly get, but a woman like her, with her beauty and social standing, could.

A supermodel superstar and a poor waitress, as if there could be any competition between us.

And then she offered to buy the restaurant.

And Cliff said he was considering it.

That was the last straw. I couldn't stay in that office for another moment, not while *she* was there or if Cliff was actually thinking of selling Rockpool. Both were too much for me to handle. I had to leave. I had to rush away.

I have to get away from him.

And that's why I'm practically running to the beach.

Why would Cliff consider selling the place?

What about us? What about everything we've built together?

None of it makes any sense. I'm so confused.

I need to get away from them.

Of course, the boy would run to the pretty girl in the end over me.

I knew that would happen. I was stupid to believe otherwise. It was stupid for me to dream and fantasize about a future together that would never be. We're all fools in love.

Love can blind us to reality.

"Bay!"

I hear Cliff's voice somewhere far behind me on the street.

"Bay!"

I pay no attention to him. I don't turn around. I don't want to see him.

He's chasing after me.

I reach the end of the main road of New Water, where the town makes its way onto the beach. I skip down the stairs into the white sands, still wearing my shoes. I don't care.

As long as I get away from him.

I wrap my arms around myself and sprint across the beach towards the cool blue water. I need to get away from Cliff.

"Bay, wait," he calls from the top of the stairs behind me.

I hope he doesn't follow.

I want to be alone.

He wants to sell Rockpool. He doesn't want to wait and see how it goes? Now I know he was lying to me, that the place wasn't a labor of love for him like he said it was. Instead, all this time he's just been waiting around to sell it? Get rid of it?

Get rid of me.

And then he'll run back into the arms of his former lover, forgetting all about our stupid little fling. I'll be nothing to him but that silly little waitress he once fucked for a few days one summer. He'll laugh about me at celebrity dinner parties in New York and London.

"Bay!"

He's getting closer to me and I'm running out of places to run to. I reach the shoreline. The water laps at my shoes. With every step, I'm sinking into the wet sand. I can't go any further.

"Bay, wait. Hold on a second."

I finally turn around to face my lover. He's caught up to me, his long strong legs able to leap further than mine.

He stands there, a few yards away on the white sand, his hand raised as if to reach out and stop me, his face solid and stern like a marble statue. His beautiful jaw clenched.

He stares at me with his brown eyes, and I know why I've fallen in love with him.

Damn it, Bay. Don't let him get to you.

He's betrayed me. He's betrayed my trust in him.

He wants to sell Rockpool. He wants his ex back.

He doesn't want me.

"What, Cliff? What is it?"

"Just stop running, Bay. Please stop, I'm getting exhausted chasing you."

"I don't want you to chase me. I want to be on my own."

"I understand."

"No, you don't. Can't you see what you've said, Cliff? You want to sell Rockpool?"

"She's offering..."

"*She?* Your ex, Cliff. She's come here, out of the blue, and wants to buy the place off you."

"She's offering a good deal, Bay. I've seen the financial records, and so have you. The restaurant can't survive."

"You need a little faith, Cliff. It might survive. We're working hard at it. Have a little hope."

"But faith and hope are too much of an ask when it comes to something like this. We need money."

"You can always turn to your family, Cliff."

"I swore to myself to never take a penny from my family when it comes to my business."

"But you were more than happy to live off your inheritance holidaying around Europe," I reply.

"That was the past," Cliff says. "I was a different guy then. This is now. I don't want my family to get involved in this. It has to be someone else to buy the place."

"Someone like your ex?"

"Yes."

I snort in derision. "I don't believe you, Cliff."

"You can have as much faith and hope as you like, but there's a high chance Rockpool's going to fail," he replies.

"It *is* going to fail without the investment we need from someone like Cleo. She's going to buy it out."

"And I'll be the first to go. Either I get fired, or I'll quit. I can't work for your ex, Cliff. Don't you get it?"

"You're definitely going to get fired." This time it isn't Cliff that speaks, but a female voice.

Cleo's voice.

She appears from behind Cliff, having followed us both down to the beach. She glides on the sand towards us.

"You'll be the first to get fired," she repeats, giving me her patronizing Hollywood smile. Behind it is hatred.

Hatred of me.

She wants me gone, and she's unafraid to say so.

Who am I dealing with here?

Cliff doesn't react to her comments. It's like he's been brainwashed by her. Corrupted by her cosmetic beauty and media-trained grace.

"Can't you see, Cliff?" I ask, my voice straining over the sound of crashing waves behind me. "Can't you see she's only back because she needs a good PR image? She's just going for you because of your family name and how nice a ring on her finger will look to her million followers on Instagram. Can't you see that?"

Cliff opens his mouth to speak, but Cleo quickly interrupts.

"This is so stupid having this... confrontation out here in public," she turns to Cliff, reaching out with her perfect hand to stroke his shoulder. "It's embarrassing. How about you, Cliff? Come back to the restaurant and we can sort out the details of my offer. You must hear them. You must hear me out on what I have to offer you."

Her eyes turn back to me, shooting daggers in my direction.

"Say no," I cry out to Cliff. "Just say no. We can make Rockpool work. Trust me."

Cliff shakes his head. His eyes drop to the ground. "I have to consider every option," he says. "I have to do what's best for the business."

And that's when I know he doesn't love me.

31

BAY

PEARL AND DAVY know something's up the minute I walk through the front door. Of course, they do. They know me better than anyone. My niece, nephew, and Fisher are sitting in the living room, watching TV together, when I pull up and enter the house.

On my way up to the door I tried to dry my eyes with the backs of my hands, but once I'm inside Pearl immediately runs up to me. "What's wrong?" she asks, her sweet voice rising. She sees the tears. She sees my red cheeks. It's like she can sense the sadness and anger emanating from me.

Davy follows his sister. He looks at me quizzically.

"What's up?" he asks.

I can't hide this from them.

Pearl tugs at my pants, her cute little face staring up at me.

"What's wrong," she repeats.

How can I really explain this to them? How can I tell them why I'm upset?

"Boy troubles," I say to them softly. I manage a smile to temper their looks at me, but it doesn't seem to affect the worried expressions on my niece and nephew.

I slump into the living room and fall down on the couch, exhausted. Fisher's attention turns from the TV and onto me whilst Pearl and Davy stand in the doorway, continuing to watch me with concerned looks.

"What's wrong, sis?" Fisher asks.

I lean back and sigh. "A lot, it seems."

"Cliff?"

I nod silently and my brother frowns.

Of course, he guesses something's up. He knows me too well. Like his kids.

Pearl rushes from the door to the couch. She forces herself to sit beside me, snuggling in against my arm. It must be an uncomfortable position for her, but she really wants to comfort me. I wrap my arm around her and pinch her adorable cheeks. She knows exactly how to comfort me right in my hour of need.

"You're my little princess," I say to her, and Pearl smiles, but her eyes betray her worry for me. She knows something's wrong, but she doesn't understand. She squeezes in tighter.

"Is it serious what's going on between you and Cliff?" Fisher asks.

"I think so."

"Do you want to talk about what's going on?"

I think about Cleo and the way she's barged straight into Cliff's and my life. Her offer to buy Rockpool and Cliff's reluctant agreement to look into his. Cliff's casual betrayal of all the work he and I have put into the place.

His rejection of me.

I slowly shake my head. "No."

"Do you want me to fight him?"

"It's not like that."

"Has he hurt you, sis?"

I roll my eyes. "Nothing like that, Fisher."

My brother reaches out and gently rubs my shoulder. "It's not my place to say anything," he softly reassures me. "But I know pain. We all do here." His eyes glance around the room at Pearl and Davy.

My nephew, taking his cue from his father, steps up beside me and hugs me. A rare display of affection from the pre-teen boy. With Pearl snuggling up against me and Davy's little boyish arms around me, I can feel the tears rising again. Tears of love.

I love everyone in this room.

They're my family.

"We can't begin to understand what you're going through, Bay," my brother continues. "But let me tell you one thing, whatever it is that's happening. Let me tell you something I've learned."

"I don't feel like a lecture, Fisher. Not right now."

"No, Bay. Listen to me," he says, eyes focusing intently on mine. "Sometimes we don't listen to our heart and what it's saying to us because it's easier, sometimes, to create a false fantasy of someone rather than to expose our emotions. We prefer to make them the villain in our story, rather than see them as the hero we need. Sometimes we never see love when we absolutely should. Trust me, I've done it, and I've regretted it."

"I don't know," I whimper, trying to hold back the tears.

I think of Cliff. The last few days we've spent together. The best days of my life. I've never known happiness like it.

And now it's all gone in the blink of an eye.

"What you have," Fisher whispers. "What you have, Bay, between you and Cliff, is something special."

"Yeah?" I *crave* reassurance. I'm so weak. So vulnerable in this moment.

"I've seen it with my own eyes," my brother says. "All of us here have. We've seen how you've changed in a few days, Bay. How you've grown so much in such a short amount of time. How happy you are."

"I *was* happy, but now he's gone from me."

"In the last few days, you've been the happiest I've ever seen you, the happiest the kids have seen you."

"And now it's gone. He's gone."

"Listen to me, Bay. What you have with Cliff reminds me of what I had with my wife." Fisher nods at Pearl and Davy. "What I had with their mother. That's what you and Cliff's relationship reminds me of."

"What you two had was something magical, Fisher. No one could have that," I reply.

It's impossible that he's comparing Cliff and me to him and Pearl's mom.

But I know it's true. It is the same kind of love. True love.

"You do. With Cliff. Believe me."

"No way."

"We had true love, and that's what I see with you and Cliff. It's rare, Bay. So rare. When you find it, you've got to hang onto it, trust me. You've got to fight for it."

"Fight for it?"

"Yeah, fight for love, Bay. Especially when it's something like what you and Cliff have."

Davy nods, following his father. "Yeah," he says. "Fight for it."

Pearl buries her face into my arm. She yells out with a lungful of air. "Fight for it!"

I want to deny it, but something deep within my body

tells me that Fisher's right. I have found true love. Even though it's only been a few days, what I have with Cliff is similar to what my brother had with his wife. I know it to be true.

It's all I've ever really wanted, love like Fisher's.

And now I see he is right.

I've got to fight for it.

Fight for the love I've found.

Fuck it.

"I will," I say, and the room erupts in cheers.

32

CLIFF

"So," Cleo says, tracing her finger around my shirt's collar. "What do you think of my offer?"

I take in a deep breath.

"Well," I reply, leaning against my desk. She's right up against me. It's like Cleo's got me pinned down in here in the manager's office, trying to make it seem like I can't escape from her grasp. "It sounds alright, but I'll need to think on it."

"Of course."

"But Rockpool does need an investment," I reply.

"Yes, it does. You're lucky I'm here. It'll have already collapsed if I didn't fly in."

"Sure."

"Don't worry," Cleo coos, patting me on the cheek. "Don't fret. I'll keep you as co-owner, but that means you won't have to be here often. Actually, that means you won't have to be here at all. We'll hire someone to take care of this place, a professional restauranteur from Sydney or

Melbourne, perhaps? I can afford them. That means you can spend more time with me."

"Is that your deal?"

Cleo chuckles. "Oh, yes. That's *my deal.*"

"Anything else to it?" I ask.

There's always more with Cleo.

"Of course, we'll have to get married, and soon. My first Vindicator movie comes out next year, and I'll have to have the ring on my finger well before then."

Ah, I knew she'll talk about a wedding sooner or later.

But this is exactly what I wanted in the Paris hotel room, exactly what I wanted when I went on my knees in front of her in that luxury suite.

Why would I be afraid of her talking about it now?

But it's like our marriage is part of this deal to take Rockpool off my hands. It's like I'm being used.

"Married?" I ask.

Cleo smiles. "I was thinking somewhere back home for the celebration. New York? Or maybe Los Angeles. We'll invite a lot of other famous people, and you can get your family to bring in all their big business pals. I'm sure you have a lot of connections in the States that would *kill* for an invitation to this wedding."

I don't know how to reply. My mind's a mess.

"Right."

"And, naturally, we'll hold it somewhere glamorous, somewhere perfect for Instagram," she says.

What?

"Instagram?" I blubber out.

"Of course," Cleo sighs, like I've said something stupid. Like she's talking to a child. "We've got to have the press on board for our little ceremony. Well, it's not exactly a *little* ceremony. I'm actually planning something quite big, aren't I?" She giggles at her own comment, but I'm not really listening anymore.

Instagram? The press? Celebrities?

This isn't what I've wanted. But seeing the greedy glint in Cleo's eye, I know it's what she wants.

She wants something completely different from me.

When she speaks about New York and extravagant parties, I'm reminded of something - *someone* - very different.

Bay Dover.

I'm reminded of the last few days together, and all we've done together. Us two being a little team. The little life we've shared in the last few days and what we could see in the future together. Running a new Rockpool in this sleepy small town. Surfing. Living the simple, quiet, and rewarding life.

That's what I really want.

Not international weddings and social media and Paris suites and diamonds.

Just Bay Dover and I working hard together.

That's what I truly want.

I bared my soul to Bay, and she didn't laugh at me as Cleo had done back in Paris. She didn't laugh at my exposed emotions or my sincerity. In fact, she embraced me for it. She made me a better man in all the time I've spent with her.

I feel for her deeper than I ever had with Cleo, or even with any other girl.

The beach today. The way I threw away her feelings. The way I treated her. That wasn't me; that was the self-obsessed Cliff Finn from a year ago. The Cliff who fucked and dumped supermodels. I'm different now. Bay has *made* me different.

On the beach today I hurt her.

I hurt the woman I love.

Oh god, what have I done?

Cleo's still talking. With her long sharp fingernail, she's driven me against the office desk, like she's a bird of prey trapping her next victim. "I've got a lot of ideas for the wedding I can run past you," she says. "I've made a collage of my vision for the day. Oh, by *run past you*, I mean I've already made up my mind. I just want to show you what I think our wedding will be like. I can see it already. It'll be the exclusive event of the year."

"Stop," I command, brushing her finger off my chest and standing up straight in front of the actress. "That's enough."

Cleo laughs at me. It's the same laugh she did back in that Parisian hotel room. A laugh of derision. "What're you doing, Cliff?" she asks, snorting through her nose at me.

"I've changed my mind, Cleo," I reply. "I've decided to keep the restaurant."

"What are you talking about?"

"I don't want your money. I'm going to keep this place."

"You can't be serious."

"Bay and I have faith it'll work out."

"*Bay?*" Cleo snorts again at the name. "That girl? The one who threw a temper tantrum on the beach?"

"Yeah, her. *That girl.*"

Cleo stands up straight. She scans me up and down like I'm insane, but I know I'm not.

This is the most clear-minded I've been for a very, very long time.

"Rockpool will fall apart without my money," she says, her voice low.

"We don't need your money," I reply. "We've put a lot of work into this place. A lot of love. I'm planning to see it through."

"Trust me, this place will collapse in a week. Just you wait."

I shake my head. "I'd rather have this place collapse a thousand times over than go through a single wedding to you."

Cleo's eyes widen and she involuntarily takes a step back. "What?" she shrieks.

"You heard me."

There's a long pause as she digests this information.

And, judging from the expression on her face, she really doesn't like it.

Cleo huffs, scans me up and down one last time in disdain, then storms out of the manager's office.

33

HALF AN HOUR EARLIER

BAY

I'VE PROMISED my family that I'll fight for Cliff and mine love.

I promised.

And I'll deliver.

That's what led me out of that living room, out of Fisher's house, into my car, and straight to the restaurant with the cheers of my brother and his kids still ringing in my ears.

I arrive at Rockpool to hear animated voices coming from the manager's office. It's like that time before when I heard Dominika talk about her father's passing, and, just like that one time, I sneak up to the doorway and put my ear up to the door, listening intently.

The voices are loud.

It's Cliff. I easily recognize his strong cadence.

And then there's someone with a silk voice. Sultry.

Cleo Dash.

She's here. At Rockpool.

They must still be talking about this deal she's offering him for the restaurant.

Oh, no.

I know it's rude, but I have to listen to this. Curiosity got the better of me.

I strain to hear them through the closed door.

"I just want to show you what I think our wedding will be like." It's Cleo.

Our wedding?

So, she wants to get married to Cliff. Do what he tried to do months ago. She *wants* him, even if she rejected him only weeks ago.

Just then I promised my family I'll fight for what I have and now I will. I looked into Pearl's eyes back at the house and told her I am going to go back to the restaurant and get what is mine. My relationship. Cliff and I's relationship. And I'm not going to let my niece down.

This is my fight.

Love can blind you to what's in front of you, but love is blinding me no more.

"I've changed my mind, Cleo. I've decided to keep the restaurant."

Cliff.

Yes, he still believes in this. In us. My heart leaps in my chest.

I still have hope.

"Bay and I have faith it'll work out."

Faith.

That's what I told him he needed, just a bit of faith and hope.

"I'd rather have this place collapse a thousand times over than go through a single wedding to you."

"What?"

"You heard me."

The words are coming thick and fast.

I need a moment to wrap my head around this.

Cliff's rejecting Cleo.

He's rejecting her for *me?*

There's a lump in my throat.

I knew it. I knew our relationship was stronger than his past, stronger than my fears, stronger than any obstacle set in our way.

But before I can truly comprehend what this means, I hear shoes scraping the floor. Someone's storming towards the office door and coming straight for me.

I stand up and take a step back, pretending I've just walked into the restaurant. I don't want to appear suspicious.

Cleo slams open the door and rushes into the main part of the restaurant. Seeing me, her face turns into a violent snarl. She glares at me up and down as if I'm a rodent in her way, and then brushes past me towards the exit.

Even with her disgusted look, I have a feeling that something's changed in the air between us in those brief moments she passes me on the way out. She's no longer the untouchable superstar and I'm the lowly waitress. Instead, it's like the tables have turned on us. She's lost something now. I'm somehow above her.

And it's all to do with Cliff.

With Cleo gone in a huff, I rush into the manager's office. I'm breathless. My body's on fire inside. My mouth is dry.

I need to see him.

"Bay?" Cliff's face is a mixture of surprise and relief at the sight of me. And something else. Something like... *joy.*

"Cliff."

"What are you doing here?"

I'm so overcome with energy that I let out everything in one long unbroken string of words. I can't help myself. "I've overheard what you two were talking about. I'm sorry, I just entered, and I heard voices. I heard the end of what you were talking about and then she... Cleo's left."

Cliff nods slowly. "She has."

"I overheard it all."

"You did?"

"I did."

I see Cliff's eyes fill with tears. I've never seen this kind of emotion from him. He leaps towards me, across the office, and takes me in his arms, hugging me close against his firm chest. I'm overcome by his sudden embrace. It was surprising, but so, so welcome. "I'm sorry," he whispers into my ear. "I'm sorry for saying what I said. I'm sorry for even contemplating selling Rockpool. I'm sorry for even speaking to *her*."

He's speaking the truth.

"No, Cliff," I reply into his shoulder pressing against me. "I'm sorry for being so out-of-control. I was just afraid of losing you."

"I've been afraid too. Afraid of losing you as well."

"And what about this place?" I ask.

"Heck, I'm *still* afraid of losing this restaurant."

"I'm afraid of that too, but we can just work hard. We can do this together."

"But I'm not afraid of one thing," Cliff says, his voice rising. "I'm not afraid of what I feel anymore. Bay, I love you."

I gasp.

I knew, deep down, that was true.

I also know one other thing.

"I love you," I reply.

I know that completely.

34

THREE MONTHS LATER

BAY

THE RESTAURANT IS THRIVING.

We're full, and it's a Monday night, what should be the quietest night of the week and *we're full*.

I'm busy cooking food in the kitchen, my hands dancing from pan to stove to dish, serving up amazing food. I take a peek out of the pass to double-check on the front of house.

Yeah, the restaurant is packed out.

The coolest spot in New Water. The hippest joint in town.

And it's all down to Cliff and mine hard work these last few months.

Oh, and someone else's hard work as well.

Dominika.

She's in the kitchen next to me. She came back a few weeks after our re-opening, her family well-taken care of back in Europe. She walked through the front doors of Rockpool one sunny afternoon and asked for her job back.

Cliff and I had no choice but to take her back because she never lost that job.

It was always waiting for her.

Neither Cliff nor I have seen Cleo Dash since she stormed out of Rockpool. She's now engaged to some famous bodybuilder, someone who's as equally into posing for selfies on Instagram as she is.

I hope she's happy. I've got nothing against her.

I've found my happiness, and it's here. In this kitchen. In this restaurant with Cliff Finn.

"Try this," Dominika forces a cooked prawn under my nose, her soft Polish accent a reassuring voice in the busy kitchen.

"Alright." I bite down on the food. "Wow, Dominika. That's delicious."

She doesn't reply beyond a cheeky wink before she's back hard at work in her section.

We need all hands on deck tonight.

Our tables are packed out.

The kitchen doors burst open and in strolls Cliff, his muscular arms pushing aside the swinging doors with ease.

"Hey girls," he says as he enters with that cocky swagger of his.

"Hey, Cliff," Dominika replies. "Stay out of our way if you know what's good for you. We're cooking up a storm here."

"I don't doubt you are."

"What do you want?" I ask him as I wipe down a plate.

Cliff gestures with a finger for me to come over. "Bay, I need you."

I nod at the plate I'm currently serving up. "I'm busy."

Cliff smiles. "The interview's here."

Oh, right. The interview.

Can't miss that.

"I'll be out in a second," I say, rushing over to the sink to wash my greasy hands.

I follow Cliff into the manager's office. Sitting in front of the desk is a young woman, around twenty. Blonde hair and a sweet smile. Her eyes flicker between Cliff and me, clearly nervous.

"Hi, I'm Bay," I say, shaking her hand as I enter. I double-check there's no leftover grease from the kitchen still on my fingers before I touch her.

"I'm Opal," she replies.

"Let's get started then, shall we?" Cliff says, sitting down in the manager's chair, commanding the room like he's some Mafia boss. I roll my eyes at him and he winks back at me. He thinks he's so *cool*. "So, you want to be a waitress here at Rockpool? Why?"

The girl seems alarmed by his intense interrogation.

"Ignore him," I whisper to the girl. "He's a brute."

"Don't worry," she replies with a flash of her white teeth. "I've dealt with some brutes in my time."

I laugh, and Cliff's cheeks go red.

"I like her already," I say to him.

I know right then we're gonna hire her. I know this new girl will fit in well here at Rockpool. If she's able to fight back against Cliff like she's just done, then she's exactly the type we're looking for.

I take in a deep breath before I launch into the interview proper.

And I know everything's going to be good.

EPILOGUE

BAY

"They're cute, aren't they?" Ripley asks me, nodding towards the men playing with Pearl and Davy in the surf.

"Who? The guys or the kids?" I joke.

Ripley and Sandy giggle at my comment as we stand on the sand, enjoying the setting sun over the waves.

"Both," Sandy replies.

We turn back to watching Cove, Skipper, and Cliff playing with Pearl and Davy in the ocean. The kids scream in mock terror as Cliff tackles them in the surf as the waves crash around them. Cove's holding a surfboard above his head. The men had tried teaching my niece and nephew to surf, but it's descended into pure chaos. Pearl was more keen to splash Cove and Skipper with water than to bother standing on the surfboard, and Davy was eager to wrestle with Cliff, thinking that he might be stronger than the six-foot-something man. He was very wrong.

They all are cute.

My heart beats stronger in my chest as I stare out at them all playing together. One big happy family.

Pearl and Davy may have sadly lost a mother, but they've gained a family.

The last few weeks have been life-changing for them. Sandy, as head of Poseidon's Academy, has been able to enroll them on a full scholarship to the elite private school. No doubt helped by Skipper's influence on the school's board. My niece and nephew are going to get the education they deserve. Fisher was overcome with emotion when he heard the news. He disappeared from the house for a whole evening when I told him. I knew where he went, though. I know that he was talking to his wife at the cemetery, telling her the good news.

She would be proud of her husband. She would be proud of her kids.

The group heads onto dry land, away from the ocean, and towards us girls on the beach. The men are topless. Perfect examples of finely toned abs and wet, firm torsos. Cliff's carrying Pearl under one arm effortlessly. He's so strong. My niece giggles as she's carried in.

I love seeing Cliff like this.

He'll make a perfect dad.

The men head straight up to us, with Davy chasing behind. Cliff gently drops Pearl to the ground, and she squeals in excitement. She loves how he carried her.

"Hey boys," Ripley says, flicking back her hair. Cove picks her up in his arms and kisses her passionately on the lips. Skipper, afraid of being outdone, does the same with Sandy. The girls laugh and kiss their men back.

I watch Cliff as he checks to see everyone's here, then he kneels down in front of me in the sand.

"What are you doing, Cliff?" I ask, concerned at what he's doing. "Are you alright?"

Why is he in the sand? Why is he kneeling?

"Bay," he says. "I need to ask you a question."

I quickly catch on to what he's doing, and I gasp and cover my mouth with my hands.

The others stop and turn, shocked.

We all know what Cliff's doing.

He smiles at me.

His gorgeous cocky smile.

"Will you marry me?" he asks.

It doesn't take me more than a second to answer. I know what I'm going to say. I've always known what I'm going to say.

"Yes."

Elated, Cliff jumps to his feet and picks me up in the air. I spin above him in his strong arms. The others cheer. I see Sandy and Ripley smile. I see Cove and Skipper roll their eyes at Cliff's display.

I see my niece and nephew open their mouths with glee.

I look into Cliff's eyes and see the joy in them.

And I know I have the same expression.

And I can't believe it.

I'm going to marry Cliff Finn.

My Superman.

ABOUT THE AUTHOR

Rebecca has had the storytelling bug since... forever!

What Rebecca likes most is writing steamy hot filthy romances with sweet happy endings sprinkled with some delicious bad boys.

Born and raised in an Aussie coastal town, she loves travelling around the world - meeting new people and discovering their stories.

Aside from adventuring she also enjoys a good rainy day in with a good book or at a hot beach catching the sun.

She's a world-class napping professional. You'll most likely find her asleep snuggled up on a sofa somewhere cozy.

For other titles and information please visit
rebeccacastle.com

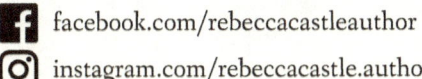

facebook.com/rebeccacastleauthor
instagram.com/rebeccacastle.author